THE STACK

C.C. LUCKEY

First paperback edition October 2020

Front cover art by C.C. Luckey

ISBN 978-1-7341281-4-7 (paperback)
ISBN 978-1-7341281-5-4 (ebook)

Published by Colleen C. Luckey

PROLOGUE - THE WAPITI OF 1969

The desperate, fists-on-wood noise that had disrupted the forest all afternoon finally stopped.

Whoever was making the banging sound didn't stop because they had succeeded in some particular goal, or because anyone had interrupted them. A thin, desperate wailing rolled through the woods, high and mournful, cracking at the peaks before running out of breath at the bottom. It was the cry of the defeated. Whoever made the noise had only stopped because they had given up.

In the flourishing forest on a hot summer night, natural silence reigned. There were birds, and some bears, and one especially large wapiti with unsettling red eyes and mold on its antlers. But traffic noise, there was not.

Now, ten minutes shy of midnight, the forest was as still as it had ever been. It waited. It knew what was coming, and it waited.

In the night sky the clouds parted, clearing a path for the full moon to drench the house's flat roof in a milky layer of secondhand sunlight. Moss grew there, living an easy life among the puddles that formed after every spring drizzle. At the edges of the odd roof, nighttime dew collected in fat drops that marched in rows down the eaves to plummet into little holes eroded deep in the mud.

The summer solstice had arrived. Fresh sprigs of grass, newly coaxed from the warming earth by the midsummer sun, glowed in the moon's blue light. Soon the lingering coldness of the pleasant spring nights would surrender their hold on the days and give way to afternoon hours that better retained the heat. A single hour of cozy mid-afternoon warmth would expand to a healthy duration of intense California swelter, blooming flowers on the plants which would dry and wither in the fall, providing fodder for the autumn fires. But for now, summer's prime was right around the corner.

This year, the house would not survive to witness the change.

At two minutes to midnight, the wailing inside the house ceased. From the edge of the forest stepped a wapiti. If any residents from nearby Downieville had been standing witness to the giant elk's arrival, they would have gasped and fumbled for a camera. Myths surrounding the wapiti had been a town staple for over a hundred years, but few pictures had even been taken of the beast. Some persistent photographers had captured the tips of its antlers disappearing behind a tree, or a flash of white from its rump, but none had ever managed a clear shot of its red-tinged eyes. Not one.

It raised its head, flaring its nostrils. Smoke was in the air. Someone was burning something.

The windows of the house flickered, too bright for the light of a fireplace. The curtains were engulfed, scorching the glass panes with black ash. Flashes of light traveled through the house from room to room as whoever was inside lit each section ablaze with methodical determination. Behind the window of the final room the figure paused, and touched the torch to its chest. Despite the action having clear intent, it was unable to control its agonized thrashing as the fire spread across its skin, eating its clothes, disintegrating its hair.

Thirty seconds to midnight.

The wapiti watched the house burn with indifference. The resident's actions mattered little. All would move ahead as planned, as it always had, as it always would.

In preparation for the main event, the wapiti shook its

head and assumed a different shape. It reared up, kicking its hooves, and as it rose it transformed. At five seconds to midnight, the creature which was not an elk stood with the legs of a human male, muscled and powerful, six feet tall—or nine feet tall, if you took into account the antlers still fixed on its skull. It crouched in the new grass, digging its fingers deep into the wet earth.

It was time.

The ground first shook gently, then began to roll. Fir trees creaked and trembled. A few lost their weaker branches. Pine cones worked free of their stems and fell, rattle and snap, to the mat of green needles which covered the forest floor.

As the earthquake intensified, the elk-man's eyes blazed. They turned a bolder shade of red, bright enough to cast a bloody glow on the ground, creating a halo around his body. He spread his legs, finding a stronger purchase on the rolling earth, and groaned with delight.

Windows which had not yet been cracked by the fire blew out, showering glass and sparks away from the sides of the house in a spray of fireworks. The figure inside had stopped moving; a temporary condition, to be sure. It had made no trouble for anyone but itself, and it would suffer for its carelessness when it awakened. It had made a poor choice.

The shaking became stronger yet. A full-sized tree fell over somewhere deep in the forest, taking the limbs of its neighbors down with it. Topsoil shifted on the hillside where the roots of spring's youngest sprouts were not yet deep enough to hold it in place. Pebbles tumbled in small falls down the slope behind the house, and larger rocks bumped away from the sides of their dirt beds, threatening to roll into the yard.

As the earthquake peaked, the house started to sink.

Its moisture-stained walls descended, burying first the street number which was painted in delicate swooping text near the front step. The cobblestones on the path were then buried, along with a lawn gnome and a garden hose. Even the shrubs lining the walk crumbled into the earth, as if the soil had turned to lava.

Clods of dirt cracked and broke away from the exterior walls like a puzzle undone. The ground approached the sills of the shattered front windows, and the house looked back at the elk-man in its plight, pleading, an unskilled swimmer sinking in deep water. But the man stood by as sand poured in through the open holes, tumbling over furniture, knocking over lamps. Inside the house, a fall of earth covered the burning resident's body, dousing the flames which had eaten away its flesh. Yet still it writhed in agony, despite its death.

The fire was out, but smoke continued to pour from the windows until the eaves touched the ground. The pressure of the rising earth popped the rain gutters off their moorings but they were quickly devoured as well, as the ground rose over the errant strips of plastic and buried them in tidy grave mounds.

In minutes, nothing remained but a thin smokestack sticking up above the disrupted soil, until it too was toppled and eaten by the earth.

When the last tiny scrap of the structure had been swallowed by the hungry ground, the shaking stopped. The trees of the forest were born anew, scrubbed clean by the shaking, now free of rotten branches and last season's pine cones. And the lot was empty; an enticingly empty clearing, just begging for something to be built.

It would be a lovely spot for a home.

The elk-man, satisfied, started to dig. He flung handfuls of dirt out behind, lowering himself into the ground.

His downward progress was faster than his hands could have achieved on their own; the earth was helping him. It eagerly engulfed him, absorbing him into its womb.

The forest settled, quiet again, now on the far side of the solstice. The hard part was done, the work was over. Warm days lie ahead, and the woods waited with held breath, full of eager anticipation.

CHAPTER 1

"I can't believe it. I just can't."

Max slumped into his beloved recliner, which made a rusty squeak. It had been a first-anniversary gift from Emily years ago, in what felt like another lifetime. She had saved up for months, tucking the money away in an old jewelry box—the kind with the little ballerina that flipped up and danced when you opened the lid. Three hundred dollars she'd saved up. That was enough for the chair, tax, and delivery. When he walked through the door after work on Christmas Eve, 1972, there it sat; a hundred-pound behemoth of brown corduroy and metal mechanisms, ugly as sin but too comfortable to resist. He'd loved it seven years ago, and he still loved it today.

Now the arms were worn nearly through, and the seams were rough where they had popped and been restitched and popped again. Max had replaced the foam in the arms once, and in the seat twice. Coffee stains adorned the left side, and a cigarette burn laid bare the stuffing on the right. Still, the chair had outlasted his marriage.

"What can't you believe?"

Penny had just walked in the front door. She unshouldered her backpack and tossed it into the corner of the entryway. Her braids had sprung errant floating hairs under the pressures of a full day of middle school.

"Nothing," Max said, tucking the notice into his shirt pocket. The bad news could wait until after dinner. Or even tomorrow. Maybe they could head up to the lake, catch some fish, and he could break the news to her there.

"Hmm. If you say so. What's for dinner?"

"I made pork chops, and there's salad left over from

yesterday. Wash your hands and we'll eat right away. I have to head to the store."

"I'll stay here while you go, okay? I have homework."

"No deal."

"But Dad…"

"I said no deal. Last week I left you here alone and we ended up with a sixty-dollar phone bill."

Penny slumped into a dining chair, scowling. "That won't happen again. Luke doesn't even talk to me anymore, anyway."

"Even so," Max said, "You're coming along. Wash up and eat. The store closes in an hour."

The winding road that was the apartment complex's only outlet to the rest of the world had seen its fair share of accidents over the years. Back in 1969, a pickup truck full of high school football players had shot over the cliff at fifty miles per hour. The sole survivor lost an arm and his license—he had been the driver, full of beer and swagger after a big win. In 1971, the year Max had moved into the place, an elderly man took a turn too fast in a storm and slid sideways into a tree, which stopped him from going all the way down the cliff but smashed his old bones to smithereens. And of course, in 1972, Penny's mom had her accident. Of course, it wasn't exactly an accident, was it? From a certain perspective, she'd been asking for it. But it was a teenage driver that had paid the price.

Max shook his head, longing for the day when he could drive down Skyline Drive without thinking about those rough times. Maybe the notice was a good omen; maybe being forced out of the apartment was just what he and Penny needed. This old town held too many painful memories. Penny wouldn't like switching schools, if it came to that. He'd try to find a new place in town, but if he couldn't—if they had to move far away from here—well, maybe that was just fate letting him know it was time to move along down the road.

After Penny finished her dinner and re-braided her hair, they buckled into Max's old Ford station wagon. The car was a pleasant shade of green, and handled like a dream. The old girl was reliable, too, despite what she'd been through. She had even survived his ex-wife's reckless driving.

Greg's Grocery was little more than a glorified liquor store, but Max did most of his shopping there anyway. They had bread and cheese and a small selection of local produce. Penny got most of her lunches at school, so that kept his cooking duty down to a minimum. The place met his needs, and would be one of the few things he'd miss if they ended up moving away.

"Max! How's life treatin' ya?" Greg nodded from his post behind the counter.

"Fine enough," Max said, nodding back. "Just here for a paper."

"We got one or two left. Sale on onions, too, if you're interested. Local grown."

"Hmm." Max's experience cooking onions for a fussy eleven-year-old was minimal. What could you make with onions? Soup, probably. Ten to one odds she wouldn't like it, and he'd be stuck eating onion soup for the next week.

"Buy the onions, I'll throw in the paper," Greg offered.

"What the heck, I'll take a bag."

Greg nodded, and procured the produce and paper from behind the counter. "That'll be seventy cents."

Max fished coins out of his pocket as Penny wandered through the store in the direction of the cosmetics aisle. When she had moved out of earshot, he leaned on the counter. "Hey, you hear of any places to rent coming up? Going to need a new spot for me and Penny by next month."

"Nope. Everything's full up, far as I know. Your rent get raised? People been in and out of here all day bitching about those notices. Seems the owners of the Skyline decided to make life hard for half your building."

Max nodded. "That's about right. I won't be able to afford the new rate. You say you heard the same from others?"

"For the last couple days. There won't be anything available in town, I'm afraid. Not with the big exodus from your building happening all at once."

"Damn."

"That what the paper's for? You looking for rental listings?"

Max nodded, but kept his mouth shut. Penny was on her way back with a bubblegum pink lipstick gripped in her hopeful hand.

"Dad, can I…"

"Sure, hon. As long as it's not 'hooker red,'" Max said, grinning.

"It says, 'Baby's Blush.'"

"Baby's butt?"

"Blush! Baby's Blush!" Penny stomped a foot and pretended to be mad. And maybe she really was, for a second, but then she laughed. She always did.

"Eleven cents," Greg said with a wink. "For the 'Baby's butt.'"

Max dumped an extra dime and penny on the counter as Penny jammed the lipstick into her pocket and stormed out of the store.

"Good luck," Greg said as Max gathered his purchases. "I'm afraid you're going to need it, Max."

Max frowned and nodded. He was afraid of that, too.

Luck wasn't one of his strengths.

Penny went to bed at 9:45, which made 10:00 the witching hour. That wasn't as bad as it sounded; Max just liked to pour out a bourbon or two once the kid was asleep. Sometimes three or four. Six on a really, really bad night.

This was one of those nights.

Was he the last tenant to receive his notice? The "*For Rent*" columns of the real estate section had been scrubbed clean of anything south of a grand per month. It was like everyone else in the Skyline had insider information on the rent increase.

Anyway, those details didn't matter much now, did they? Thirty-five days from today, he and Penny would need to be on their way out the door.

He looked around the living room. It had remained mostly unchanged since his ex-wife, Emily, had left. She had done most of the decorating, which mainly consisted of hanging up dusty purple drapes with big orange flowers, and a series of family photos marching down the hall. These walls had seen good times and bad, both before and after 1972. Once there had been a happy family of three living here, and now, in 1979, there was a happy family of two.

So, where could they go? Penny had lived in the Skyline apartment building on the outskirts of Roseville her whole life. But Roseville, like its neighbor San Francisco, was growing, and it was leaving Max's meager income behind.

He felt a pang of guilt. His job allowed him to be a stay-at-home dad, but there was never wiggle room in the budget. Maybe he should have tried harder to get a job in an office somewhere. But then Penny would be a latchkey kid, coming home from school every day to an empty house. Was that really better?

An empty house was better than none. She'd have nowhere to go home to if he didn't figure this out. Maybe she'd even have to move in with Emily. Above all else, Max could never allow that to happen.

He rubbed his face with his rough carpenter's hands, and sipped at his second bourbon. No, leaving this apartment behind was just fine by him. It would be healthy for Penny, too. And it would put to rest his memories of both the good and bad times with Emily, from carrying her through the door after they first got the key to the night when he got the call from the police station. When they told him that something had happened to his wife on Skyline Drive, and she was unconscious, and could he come advocate for her at the hospital...

Max's cheeks burned. He sniffed, wiping at his eyes. Damn, but the bourbon was strong today.

"Dad?"

He straightened up in his battered old chair. No good for Penny to see him like this. "Hon? Can't sleep?"

Penny shook her head. "No. My tummy hurts."

"Sounds like you had too many pork chops."

"More like too much salad."

"That seems unlikely. Come sit down."

Penny shuffled through the living room in her purple bunny slippers, a gift from the Easter Bunny last week. She sat and stared, wide-eyed, at Max's red face. He sighed, knowing what she saw there.

"Dad? Are you okay?"

He might as well tell her now. Whatever she might imagine was bad enough to make her daddy cry would likely be worse than the truth. And the truth wasn't so bad, after all. Probably.

"I got a letter from the apartment manager today.

They are going to raise the rent on our apartment, by a lot. A whole lot. More than I can pay."

Penny frowned, thinking. "What if I give up my allowance?"

Max smiled. "Even more than that, Penny. We're going to have to move out."

He let that sit with her for a couple minutes. She stared down at her hands in her lap, cogitating on the meaning of it all.

"Can we move into the house next to Jenny? She said her neighbors moved out and it's for sale."

Max shook his head, trying not to feel ashamed. He needed to tell her the whole truth. "I can't afford that either. I need to find a new place for us to rent, and it looks like it won't be near here. We'll have to move to another city, somewhere further away from Roseville. It's just too expensive to live here now."

"Would I have to switch schools?"

Max nodded. "Yes, I'm afraid so."

"Good."

Max raised his eyebrows, startled. "Good?"

"Then I'll never have to see Jessica again. She's a bully, and I hate her."

"Now honey, I've told you that you should never hate anyone. But yeah, it's possible that you might never see her again. A new town would mean new friends, and maybe leaving some old ones behind. You gonna be okay with that?"

Penny nodded. "I can handle it."

Max grinned. Penny was so strong. She took after all the best aspects of her mother; feisty auburn hair, thick skin, and a wanderlust Max could hardly keep up with.

"I know you can. Never doubted it."

Penny stood and leaned over the recliner, setting her

pointy chin on Max's shoulder. They hugged, awkwardly, and Penny shuffled back toward her room. Before she turned the corner to the hall, she looked back at her father and smiled. "I'm kind of excited, actually."

"Me too," Max said. "This will be an adventure."

CHAPTER 2

"**E**mily, that's not what happened. I swear to god if you try to use this against me…"

"If you're going to be homeless, Penny needs somewhere to stay. She can stay here with me and Rick for as long as she wants. He has a huge house in San Jose, and she'll have a whole big room all for herself. Don't you want her to be comfortable? Who knows how long it will take you to get this situation sorted out."

"I already have appointments to look at three different places," Max lied. "I'll get it worked out long before it becomes a problem. We won't be out on the street, Em."

There was a long pause on the other end of the line. She was probably doing mental math, trying to figure out how much it would cost to hire a lawyer and get her custody reassessed before Max could relocate to a new apartment. It wouldn't be cheap, but she loved Penny almost as much as Max did.

"We'll see," she said, sniffling.

"Allergies?" Max said with just the right level of condescension in his tone. Emily didn't have spring allergies; it was more like an affinity for winter snow.

"Yeah, sure, allergies. They're a bitch. Well, keep me updated, okay? I just want to make sure Penny stays safe." In the background, a man's muffled voice asked if she was talking to her ex-husband.

"That Rick I hear?" Max asked, knowing it was.

"Yep. We're just going to go get dinner. I'd ask you to join us, but I doubt you could afford to go dutch, and Rick's not into charity."

"That's me, piss-poor and gutter-bound. Enjoy your

filet mignon, my dear, and don't forget to wipe the powdered sugar from your nose before you head out the door."

"Fuck off, Max." The receiver switched to the open
dial-tone with a loud click.

That had gone poorly. Max had felt obligated to
update her on what was happening, but now he wasn't
so sure it had been the right move. What business was it
of hers? He had full custody for good reason. But part of
him wanted to make sure she still cared about Penny, still
felt like her daughter was a real person in her life. Maybe,
someday, she and Penny could be close again. But Emily
was the one who would have to grow up first, not Penny.

Penny was great. Sometimes just thinking about his
daughter gave him the giddy giggles. He had to find them
somewhere amazing to live, no matter what. She deserved
nothing less than the best.

He spent half the next day driving around, keeping an eye
out for any *"For Rent"* signs the rest of his evicted neighbors might have missed. There were several *"For Sale"*
signs, but nothing anywhere near his price range—which
was, essentially, zero dollars. He finally reached the outskirts of Sacramento before giving up and turning around.
Prices would only go up as the city streets grew more
dense, and he didn't want Penny growing up in that kind
of neighborhood anyway.

Penny beat him home by ten minutes. She was sitting
in the kitchen when he walked in the door, chatting on
the phone with one of her million little friends. They were
talking about moving. She waved as he walked in the door
and set down a paper bag filled with wood pieces, stain,
and glue from the Roseville hobby store.

Max eyed the candy bar wrapper on the counter in
front of Penny before she could crumple it in her fist.

Without interrupting her conversation, she grinned and shrugged. What you gonna do, Dad?

He pointed at her, then pointed at the bowl of fruit on the counter.

She rumpled her nose. Yuck.

He shrugged, then held his arms out from the sides of his body and puffed out his cheeks. You wanna get fat?

Penny shook her head and put her hand over her mouth, trying not to laugh into the receiver.

Max retreated to his small bedroom. Half of the room was bed, and half of it was workstation. There wasn't room for much else. A tidy row of miniature wooden houses lined the windowsill, ready to be stained with the new Golden Maple he had just picked up from the store. The buildings were a special order from a Mrs. Alice Crenshaw in Michigan who said she was a teacher setting up a train track for her elementary school, an educational display of the United States during the gold rush. When Max wondered why she wanted such top-quality work—he was one of the best in his field, and charged accordingly—she said the toy train set would be a permanent installment in the school's auditorium lobby, and as it was to be an educational tool, it needed to be just right. It sounded to Max more like she was trying to justify an inflated budget, but it didn't much matter to him. Tomorrow he would ship out six perfect little houses, made period-accurate to 1854.

Penny laughed downstairs, at whatever eleven-year-olds laugh at. Was she old enough to have a steady boyfriend? Probably not, but that sixty-dollar phone bill suggested otherwise.

He sat on the bed and picked up a stack of mail he had brought in with him. Bills, circulars, junk. A reminder from his dentist that it was time for a cleaning. A blue envelope with words in giant yellow print: *You've Won!* He chucked it all on the bedspread and lay back, straightening his spine until it popped, one-two-three.

Was it the witching hour yet? It was at least a four-bourbon day, after that morning's phone call with Emily. He stretched his arms out to each side, straightening his hands all the way to the fingertips. His back was sore from hunching over his tiny creations. Actually, just about everything hurt; his hands ached from sanding and painting, and his brain was tired from trying to solve his unsolvable housing problem. His heart was sore from talking to Emily.

Maybe it was a five-bourbon day.

His left hand landed on the mail again, and he picked up the top envelope. It was that blue one with the screaming yellow letters.

"What've I won?" he asked it. "A new car? Trip to Tahiti?"

A cute drawing was stamped onto the bottom left corner of the envelope. It was a quaint little house with a flat roof, trimmed with hedges and bordered by forest pines. Max sat up.

It was just the kind of place he would have described, if someone had asked him what he wanted for Penny. Tidy and neat, but out in the forest just a bit, and surrounded by nature. Modern yet relaxed. A place to grow.

His eyes watered as he looked at the tiny picture. The envelope contained nothing but lies, to be sure. No one really gave away houses for free. Anyway, he hadn't entered any contests, he was sure of that. He would remember if he had.

Well, how sure was he, really? Anything was possible, on a six-bourbon day...

He opened the envelope, giving himself a razor-thin cut along his thumb in the process. That one would sting later when he brushed stain onto the little row of historic houses, then fill in with a dark brown color that would take days to wear off.

The material inside the blue envelope reinforced what the exterior said, but with even more enthusiasm: Congratulations! You're Our Grand Prize Winner! A white sheet of paper covered in tiny letters tumbled to the bedspread. That's where the real deal was, the fine print. That's where it explained to you that you hadn't really won, that no one could really win, and that you were a damn fool for even dreaming for a moment that it could be true.

Max pinched his reading glasses from his pocket, but put them on only after first glancing quickly at his bedroom door, making sure Penny was still on the phone. It wasn't that he was ashamed of his failing eyesight, exactly—he was forty-two, after all—but he didn't want her to think of him as old just yet. Sure, he was old, because he was Dad. But he wasn't *old*-old. Not yet.

The tiny black words on the white paper didn't say he hadn't won. They said he was responsible for any necessary taxes, including property tax which would be determined after an assessment. He would provide his own insurance, and indemnify the contest sponsor from all liability. He had six months to claim his prize. And he could take a cash settlement in lieu of his new house, if he chose to.

His house.

Was this real?

His shaking hands turned the papers over and over, trying to find the catch. All he found was a name and phone number for the host company, Elkstone Giveaways. (530) 555-3509. Downieville, California.

"Penny?" he called out, trying to keep the tremble out of his voice. "No rush, but I need the phone. Just…just as soon as you're done with it."

CHAPTER 3

Elkstone Giveaways was closed for the day, but they would be open again tomorrow morning at 9:00, so please call back.

That's what the message on the line said, anyway. Max set the receiver back in its holder and sat on the barstool next to the phone, wrapping the spiral springy cord around his thumb, watching his fingernail turn white as the blood drained away. Of course they were closed. They probably didn't even exist. People didn't just give away houses.

He uncurled the cord from his finger and stood up. Time to get back to work. Mrs. Crenshaw would truly be bereft if her budget-validating miniature cabins weren't shipped out with the Pony Express first thing tomorrow morning.

Trying not to think about Elkstone Giveaways, he peeked into Penny's room. She was doing her homework.

God, she was such a great kid. More than he deserved.

He stopped at the doorway to his own lonely bedroom. It reeked of wood glue and enamel paint. That had to be some kind of carcinogenic blend of vapors, but what choice did he have? Whenever the weather allowed, he kept his window propped open, more for Penny's sake than his own. She was still a growing girl.

He pressed his hands on the door frame and straightened his aching back. Pop-pop-pop. Little explosions of pain followed by brief relief. It would only get worse as the years went by. In a corner of his mind, he worried a little about his endurance for the upcoming move. Penny would help, sure, but the heavy lifting would be up to him. He'd have to hire at least one hand, maybe two. That could get expensive.

As he mulled it over, the phone rang. He jumped guiltily, and immediately wondered why. No matter who was calling, what fault could that be of his?

"You expecting a call, Penny?"

"Nope. Prob'ly for you."

"Okay. I'll get it."

He walked back through the kitchen and rested his hand on the receiver, cursing at the hope fluttering in his chest. He had no reason to think Elkstone Giveaways would call him. Why on earth would they? He didn't leave a message, and they were closed for the day. Maybe that wasn't excitement in his chest, but a heart activity more sinister; maybe it was time to check in with the doc.

"Hello?"

"Mr. Maxwell Braun? This is Walter Puck from Elkstone Giveaways. How are you doing this evening?"

Max's runaway heart leapt to his throat, and he swallowed it back down. "Well, I'm doing fine. How are you?"

"Just great, and thank you for asking! And if I'm not mistaken, I'm about to make your day a whole lot better. You called us because you received our notice, is that right?"

"I suppose I did, but there has to be some mistake. I don't remember entering any contest."

"Well my paperwork says otherwise. But if you're not interested in the prize…"

"I'm interested." Max's hands were shaking, as though someone had tossed him a game-winning pass and he'd almost fumbled the ball.

"Great! I'm so glad to hear that. Of course, we have to offer the opportunity to forego the grand prize and take a cash offer, but we feel the house itself has far greater value than what'd you get for it on the market today. Shall we get started?"

"Started? What do you mean?"

"There's some paperwork for you to sign, and we need all your information, of course. If you'll give me permission, I'll just drop a packet in the mail. Congratulations, Max! We're so excited for you, over here at Elkstone Giveaways!"

"I…I don't know what to say. Is this for real?"

"It's really real, Max! That's just what we do at EG. We make dreams come true."

Four days later, Max dug a thick white envelope out of his mailbox. A notice was taped to the little door that said *"Mailbox Full, Please Pick Up Mail At Post Office."* The mail carrier hadn't been able to fit anything else in the box along with the contract for the house.

Max hadn't told anyone about his good fortune yet. He wanted to be sure—truly and completely positive—before saying anything, especially to Penny. The papers said the house was in Downieville, about two hours from their old place outside Roseville. Penny would have to change schools.

The contract was folded around several black-and-white Polaroid pictures of the house. It had an unusual, angular design that was a cross between modern and rustic, simple and artsy all at once. The photos were grainy, but clear enough to show the house had tall floor-to-ceiling windows in the front, a wide square door with a tiny barred window set into it at face-height, and a flat roof.

Penny went to a friend's house to spend the night, and Max spent hours poring over the papers. He considered hiring a lawyer to look everything over, but it all seemed so straightforward he wasn't sure it would do anything but empty his already-thin wallet. The papers required no payments on his behalf other than property taxes and insurance. If they were running a scam, he couldn't imagine what it would be. In the end, he signed everything with a flourish, taped it all together, and dropped it in the blue mailbox at the end of the street.

If it was a con, he was about to find out. But if it wasn't, he didn't want to waste any more time. Emily was breathing down his neck, ready to unleash her lawyers the moment Max looked anything other than perfectly stable. He couldn't give her that chance. Without Penny, he'd be lost.

When Penny came home in the morning, he almost told her. He had replaced sleep with bourbon, and had taken only one brief, aggressive nap for two hours after sunrise. In the end he managed to hold his tongue, barely.

Penny was full of stories about Jenny's cat. It was ten weeks old, just a kitten still, but "as cute as pie." Her hands were covered in tiny scratches and bite marks, and her shorts were dusted with little white hairs. "She's already taught him how to mew for food, Dad. It's the cutest damn thing!"

"Hey! No cussing, I don't care how cute the cat was."

"Sorry. But it's so great, you have no idea. She has black and white fur with this nose that's super pink but with a black spot on her little nostril."

"She does? I don't remember Jenny having any spots."

"Daaad…"

Max chuckled.

Penny sighed. "I wish I could have a pet. Why don't apartment buildings let people have pets?"

"Some of them do."

"Can we maybe move somewhere like that? Please, Dad?"

"Maybe."

Four days later, while Penny was at school, Max sat at the kitchen table with a sealed envelope sitting on the table in front of him. His hands rested on either side of it, pressed against the tablecloth. He had willed them to open the envelope, but they had not obeyed.

This was it. If the giveaway was a scam, he'd find out now. There would be a beg for money, or an ask for more info, or a blackmail threat, or a pyramid scheme.

He sipped his bourbon, paused to swish it around in his mouth, then downed the rest of the glass.

The envelope crinkled in his hands as he opened it. There was plastic inside; a little baggie. With a key. A house key.

There were photocopies of the papers he'd signed, a bundle of brochures for recommended insurance companies, and a deed.

A small smile spread across his face. Then it widened into a silly grin. A minute later he was laughing, gripping the key in his palm so tight it hurt even through his calluses. He cheered and jumped in the kitchen, rattling the glass in the windows and the dishes in the cabinets. Tears streaked down his stubbled cheeks and he danced, pumping his fist in the air.

Neighbors on all sides banged on the walls for him to stop the ruckus. He laughed again, but sat down, breathing hard. Nothing wrong with his ticker, after all; if there had been, he'd be laid out on the floor after that workout.

He was tempted to swing by the school and pick Penny up right away, pull her out of class to share the news. But he made himself wait. She would find out soon enough.

In the meantime, he had an idea.

At 2:45, the last bell rang. Max parked in front of the school in his usual spot. He always got the same spot; working for yourself from home allowed a lot of schedule flexibility, and he could usually beat the other parents to the front of the pickup line.

The younger boys filed out first, bursting to head home. Older boys and girls followed, some holding hands. Penny walked through the door with Jenny, laughing and nodding, bouncing her ponytail.

Max's heart thumped in his chest. The date was May 3, but it felt like Christmas morning.

Penny pulled on the door handle, but Max had locked it. He shook his head and pointed at the back seat. "Broken," he mouthed through the closed window.

She rolled her eyes and yanked on the back door, then tumbled onto the bench, jamming her backpack down behind the passenger seat.

"The door's broken? Seriously?"

"Yup. It's an old car." Max hid his smile.

Penny crossed her arms and sighed, looking out the window. Max peeked at her in the rear view window, and decided it was time.

"Hey, hon. Do me a favor."

"Whaaat," Penny droned, wiping sweat from her forehead.

"I think I left something in that box next to you. Will you take a look for me?"

"What do you…" Penny bounced in her seat and screamed—first with shock, then once again with joy.

She pulled the sleepy orange kitten out of the box and tucked it under her chin, squealing.

"You got me a cat!"

"Well, I got us a cat. You have to share him."

"I thought we couldn't have one in the apartment!"

"Well, we're moving anyway. So I figured…"

"But this will just make it even harder for us to find a new place to live, won't it?"

Max's smile faltered. Kids grew up so fast. She was only eleven. She should still be squealing about the kitten, not worrying about where they'd be living next month.

"Well, I found us a new place already, and they allow cats."

Penny gasped. "Really? Dad, that's amazing! Where is it?"

"Downieville."

"Oh," Penny said. Her smile hardened a little. She was thrilled about the kitten, but Max knew she wanted to stay close to her friends, despite her earlier optimism.

"I know it's further away than you wanted. That's why I got you a new friend. Will you promise to take care of him?"

Penny's smile glowed again. "Forever and ever, Dad. Thank you so much. I love you." She leaned forward and gave him a little peck on the cheek. "Best Dad ever."

"Just like my favorite coffee mug says."

Penny giggled. "I know, I got you that cup. And I meant it, too."

"So, what are you going to name him?"

Penny went quiet. This was an important decision. Max let her think about it as he took Skyline Drive up the hill, winding through the curves. He wouldn't miss this dangerous drive, that was for sure. And he wouldn't miss thinking about his ex-wife every time he took the last turn.

"He's the color of a shiny penny. But that's already my name. So I think I'll call him Copper."

"Like a police-cat."

Penny laughed. "Sure, Dad, whatever. Like a police-cat."

Copper mewed.

CHAPTER 4

Mr. Samson wasn't afraid of snow, rain, heat or sleet. He was a United States postal worker, and a damn good one.

He'd been bitten by dogs, shouted at by old ladies, and had narrowly avoided lightning strikes on more than one route in his thirty years as an official carrier. It was all part of the job, just another day down in the trenches.

He loved his career and he loved his route, for the most part. Only two things turned his stomach; people who didn't empty out their mailboxes every day, and the flat-roofed house at 23 Old Mine Road.

People who didn't empty their mailboxes didn't respect the important service provided by the USPS. The post office was taken for granted these days by people who would rather gab on the phone than send a nice, personal letter written in their own hand. There was even talk of computers becoming some sort of electronic mail relay, which Mr. Samson couldn't even begin to wrap his head around. It was already bad enough without that kind of technology. People who didn't empty their box would let the papers pile up, and if it got bad enough he'd have to take them back to the post office and hold them for in-person pickup. Made him feel like he didn't do his job right. It really stuck in his craw.

But there were a few different things wrong with the house at 23 Old Mine Road, and in general they both-ered him even more than the people who neglected their mailboxes. First, and worst, was this: The house at 23 Old Mine Road didn't receive any mail. Not a single circular, flyer, postcard, or paper. No Christmas cards, tax letters, or bills. Nothing. He'd never seen anything like it in all his years with the post office. Heck, every house should receive something, even if it was just junk. But for decades he had skipped right past the address. A couple different families had lived there over the years, but he saw little sign of them. Mostly just shadows in the windows. When someone was out and about in the front yard they might nod, but then they'd put their head down and go back inside pretty quick. Never a kind word, or even a question about where all their letters might be.

It was an odd business, and the whole thing aggravated Mr. Samson's ulcers to no end.

About every ten years, whoever lived there would move out, the house would get a new paint job and some renovation, and new people would move in. Sometimes the new owners were nice at the start, but before long they all acted the same; sullen, quiet, distant. No holiday cards for their neighborhood postal worker, either. No New Year cookies, or bonuses tucked in little envelopes with "*Thank You For Your Service*" scrawled on the flap like so many of his other, more civil clients tended to leave him. But of course why would they give him anything, if he never delivered any letters? He never had a chance to form a postal worker-postal client relationship with them. The whole situation was damn unnatural, beginning to end.

One afternoon in mid-March, he was walking his route when an unfamiliar station wagon pulled into the driveway of 23 Old Mine Road. It seemed a new neighbor was moving in.

A middle-aged man with silvering hair and a spare-tire belly got out of the driver's seat while a young girl holding an orange kitten bounced from the passenger side.

"Halloo, there!" Mr. Samson called out.

"Hello!" the man replied.

It was a rare occasion that anyone at 23 Old Mine

Road spoke to him, and he didn't want to miss his chance.

"You moving in?" Mr. Samson said.

"Yes sir, just today. You our mail carrier?"

"Sure am. Been working this beat for almost thirty years now. I think you'll love the neighborhood. It's real nice and quiet."

"Max Braun," the man said, holding out his hand.

"Abner Samson, United States Post Office letter carrier, Downieville North Branch."

The girl set the kitten on her shoulder and pulled a backpack from the sedan's back seat. Waving to Mr. Samson, she said, "I'm Penny, and this is Copper."

"Well, if you don't mind, we're going to get settled in," Max said.

"Of course, of course. Don't let me keep you. Welcome to the neighborhood!"

"Thank you. We're very glad to be here."

Mr. Samson waved goodbye, but his feet felt stuck in place. He wanted to say something to the man, warn him about the house. It was all wrong, that house. Every time a new family moved in, something got a hold on them and they changed. He wanted to tell them, but what could he say? It had to be today, and it had to be now. This might be his only chance. Sometimes the change happened quick.

He opened and closed his mouth like a fish, trying to make words. The man watched him from the corner of his eye with growing suspicion. Mr. Samson knew he should just give up and move along, yet his conscience wouldn't let him go.

"Something else, Mr. Samson?" the man asked.

"No. Yes. Just…be careful in there."

"Huh?"

"The house. It's had a lot of different people in it over the years."

"Just what the hell is that supposed to mean?"

Over Max Braun's shoulder, Mr. Samson could see the house staring at him with its big window-pane eyes. It was watching him, silently warning him not to say anything else. A cold chill started in Mr. Samson's feet and made its way up his back like a lightning strike, chattering his teeth.

"Nothing at all, really. I'm getting on in years, and sometimes I daydream, that's all. But…"

"Yes?"

"Just watch out," Mr. Samson whispered in a harsh, low voice he barely recognized as his own. It was all he could manage before turning away to shuffle down the street toward his next stop.

"Weirdo," the girl muttered as he left. Her father reprimanded her.

Mr. Samson felt the house eyeing him as he retreated. It was angry. He didn't know how he knew that, but he did. And just before he turned the corner that would put the house out of sight, he heard a massive, crackling chomp; crunching wood, breaking beams, shattering glass. He spun around, expecting to see the new residents being eaten alive—but no, they were only unloading boxes, chatting with each other, making plans. The house was placid, but still he felt that it mocked him with its big open eyes, like a schoolboy playing innocent. "No ma'am, I did not eat them, no I did not. Cross my heart, hope to die, a thousand splinters in my eyes."

"Asshole," he muttered at the empty windows.

A ray of sunlight flashed, reflecting in one of the glass panes bright enough to burn a spot into his vision. Pressing his eyelids shut, he quickly hurried down the street. Either the house was vindictive, or he was imagining things.

In either case, maybe it was time for him to finally hand in his uniform.

CHAPTER 5

Penny jumped up and down in the new living room, cheering. Her celebration scared little Copper out of his wits, sending him scampering under the kitchen table.

"Now, you still have to do all your homework," Max said. "Mrs. Livingston said she'd send along a weekly packet of reading and workbook pages through the end of the month, and then we can mail your finished work back and she'll grade it just like she grades everyone else's. So you might not be at the school, but you still need to actually do the work, Penny." He folded his arms, trying to look like a stern taskmaster. "No slacking off."

"I know, I know. But I won't have to change schools 'til next year! I get to stay home with you and Copper. It's like summer vacation has already started!"

"Well, not quite. Anyway, you'll be sick to death of being home every day by the time the new school year starts."

"Fine by me." Penny was beaming, twirling in circles around the house. Then she remembered Copper, and dragged him out from under the table. He resisted her cuddling for a moment before his sleepiness took over and he succumbed to a nap in her arms. She cooed at him in baby-speak with a soft voice, and sat in the modern leather recliner Max had picked up at the Discount Furniture Mart. He had parted ways with his old corduroy chair last week, in a fit of spring cleaning—not just cleaning his old apartment, but his whole life. He wanted a fresh start in every possible way. And the new house was the perfect place for that.

Max had never lived so close to a forest before. It

came almost up the house in the back, without even room
for a yard. A wooden porch held the trees away from
the sliding glass door that allowed access from the living
room. The front yard was wide open, with a cobblestone
path that led the way around the corner toward the back.
The driveway was circular, an incongruously formal look
for a house which managed to appear rusticly modern, or
modernly rustic. The overall impression of the building's
style was a hodgepodge, but it suited Max just fine. He was
a hodgepodge kind of guy.

And, more important than its shape or its style, it was
his. He had resisted a temptation to frame the deed and
hang it in the entryway near the door. It had his name on
it, and his name alone. No lending bank piggybacked on
that deed, no sir. It was all his, free and clear.

Of less importance, but still deeply satisfying, was
his conversation with Emily the day after he and Penny
moved in. Her tone had been light and congratulatory,
but he knew her well enough to detect the low snarl in her
tone. She didn't think he deserved such a windfall, and
maybe she was right. But the fact remained that he was in
a better position than ever to retain custody of Penny—
and really, in the end, that's what mattered most of all.

The house was big enough for Max to set up his
workshop in a separate room. No more sniffing chemicals
in his sleep, or finding sawdust in his bedsheets. He added
a layer of extra insulation to the door to prevent paint
fumes and glue vapors from permeating the rest of the
house, and installed fans in the windows to direct the bad
air outside. It was a dream setup. The other two bedrooms
were gorgeous, too. He took the smallest one as his own,
put his workshop in the middle room, and gave Penny the
master bedroom, which had a picture window and its own
private bathroom. She was growing up, and needed the

space more than he did.

Penny was elated, and promptly painted her bathroom Baby's Blush pink.

It took only a week to settle into the new house. Boxes
were all unpacked, everything was in its place. There
were no unused spaces in the house, and everything they
owned fit perfectly in its spot. It felt like the house was
made for them.

"Have you walked into the forest yet?" Max asked
during dinner. "If you do, watch where you step. There
will be a lot more wildlife here than there was near the old
apartment. There could even be snakes."

"I haven't gone out yet, but I'll be careful. Do you
think I could build a treehouse?"

"Maybe. Those trees are old, and the branches are
pretty high off the ground. Might be tough. But I bet we
could figure it out."

The phone rang. Max's heart leaped with surprise; no
one else had this number yet, and he hadn't expected any
calls. He had just set up the line that afternoon. Perhaps
something had already gone wrong with the deed transfer,
or the whole thing had been a scam after all. Perhaps...

"Penny, if you're done with your dinner, go to your
room and do your homework."

"'Kay." She put her dish in the sink and made her way
toward the hall, clicking her tongue for Copper to follow.

He calmed his racing thoughts, and picked up the
receiver.

"Max?" The voice on the line was familiar. "This is
Walter Puck from Elkstone Giveaways."

Max's chest pounded. He had no reason to be worried
the house would be taken away. He had the deed, with his
name written right on it. Still, his vision began to blur.

"How can I help you, Walter?" He spoke the words through numb lips.

"I just wanted to give you one last call, make sure you're settling in all right. How's the house treating you?"

"Oh, it's just great! We absolutely love it, couldn't be happier."

"Wonderful! I am so glad we-TCHHKK."

Max held the receiver away from his ear. The burst of static had been loud enough to hurt his eardrum. "Walter? You still there?"

"Sorry about that, Max. Some days are easier than others, aren't they?"

"Well, sure, I guess that's true for just about everyone."

"Some days are six-bourbon days."

Max held the receiver away from his ear again. He stared at it without comprehension, as though it had tried to bite him. Six-bourbon days. He'd never said those words out loud, as far as he knew. It was one of those funny little things that go through your head, the kind of private conversations you have with yourself to help the world make sense.

"Max? You there?"

"Yes. I'm here," Max said. He lifted the receiver to his ear but did not touch it to his head. He was afraid it would shock him if it got too close.

"Well. I'm very glad-TCHHKK-settling in so nicely. I'll give you a call back next-TCHK."

"That'd be fine, Walter. I'll talk to you later. Thanks again for everything."

Max didn't wait for a reply, but in the second before the receiver clicked down on its base, a supernatural wail rang out from the tiny speaker. It was a nasal, screeching howl, a hundred layers deep. Like a legion of trumpets from Hell, or perhaps a mortally injured moose screaming its final breath.

His heart was pounding again. What was that? What the hell had just happened? Superficially, it was just the nice man from the contest agency checking up. Nothing unusual about that. Still, it was one of the strangest phone calls Max had ever had in his life.

Max aimed a bottle at a glass and took himself out to the back porch. It was just a little strip of decking, extending no further than four feet off the back wall before the trees rushed up to challenge it. Just enough room for a chair and a little table and a charcoal grill. It was perfect, really; no muss, no fuss.

He sipped his drink, and something brushed against his lip. A tiny fir-tree seed had landed in the glass. It looked like a baby pine cone, reddish-tan and fuzzy. He picked it out and flicked it over the deck banister, then leaned back, gazing up at the sky through the branches overhead.

That flat roof would be some maintenance. Who built a house with a flat roof in an area with overreaching trees and annual snow? Ah, well. Beggars can't be choosers. More concerning was the faint odor of fire that occasionally breezed through the house. It must have burned, sometime in the past. No sign of fire damage now, though. Everything was just fine now.

Through the walls, he heard Penny laugh. Her homework was finished, and she was chasing Copper up and down the hall. She'd been spending less time on the phone in the last week, ever since they had arrived at the new place. It seemed she was moving on, too.

A high, thin cry echoed through the forest. It was squeaky and pained, a creature begging either for relief or for death. Max shuddered. The house was in the middle of a lot more raw nature than he was used to. He set his drink

on the table and stood up, peering into the forest as the cry
rang out again. His feet tingled, wanting to run away from
the sound, or from the pain the screeching spoke of. But
there was something wrong with that cry, a voice that was
twisted and textured. It was similar to the strange sound
he had heard on the phone as he hung up.

Just what the hell was happening, here?

At the top of the slope behind the house, a tree shook.
Thousands of needles worked loose from their moorings
and trickled down to the forest floor like a rain of spears.
A creature had struck the tree; dark and amorphous and
sixteen feet tall from the tips of its antlers to its hooves
on the ground. It was just a silhouette until it turned and
looked at Max, and he saw that its eyes were red as glowing embers. There was something wrong with its pupils,
too, some kind of mutation. They were in the shape of
perfect, four-sided diamonds. After the animal had taken
his measure, it turned, flashing a white rump that was
streaked with red.

Either it was female, or it was shitting blood.

Max didn't stick around to find out which. He
scooped up his glass and slammed the sliding door shut
behind him, flicking off the living room light switch with
his pinky finger without spilling his drink. He stood in the
darkening room, staring with wide eyes at the ridge on the
edge of the property.

So the house wasn't perfect. It had mad elk running
about. In a way, it was a relief. It had to be something,
didn't it? Nothing was really perfect, nothing was really
free. He could deal with a little crazed wildlife in exchange
for a nice home, no problem.

Tomorrow, he'd look into getting some fencing
installed. It would be expensive, but it had to be done, because this was his castle now. And finally, for the first time

in his life, he felt like a king.

CHAPTER 6

Electric-blue plastic ribbons marked the house's property line on the three sides that ran through forest. Max walked the perimeter with Penny trotting along behind, slipping on the slick pine needles that littered the ground.

"Yee-ow! A needle went right though my shoe!" Penny sat down against a tree, plucking a brown stick out of the toe of her canvas slip-on.

"I told you to wear your rain boots."

"But that would be weird. It's not raining."

"Okay, but you wouldn't have a hole in your toe right now, either."

Penny pulled off her shoe and examined the tiny dot on her skin. "Should've worn socks, too, I guess." A bead of blood was forming next to her toenail.

"What do you think of this one?" Max pointed at a soaring redwood with upward-angled branches like an upside-down peace sign. "The central branches there will give us something to build off of, and it's only about forty feet away from the house."

Penny pulled her shoe back on and circled the tree. She looked up at the canopy, judging its spread, and laid her hand flat on its trunk. "What do you think, tree? Want to be friends?"

"If you like this one I can pick up some wood next week, and a bucket of nails. I bet we can build the whole treehouse in three or four days, tops."

"Nails? Do we really have to bang nails into the poor tree? There has to be another way."

"Well, I suppose we could dig holes, pour some cement, and just use the tree as a brace. It would mean installing crossbars to rest on the branches, and putting poles in the ground to hold it all up. Would be a lot easier to use nails, though. And if we use poles, it wouldn't exactly be a treehouse."

Penny looked sad. "Well, I don't want to hurt the tree. I guess I don't really need a treehouse that bad, after all."

Max sighed. "All right, all right. We'll do it the hard way."

Penny beamed, and wrapped her arms around the tree's rough trunk.

Max went all-out on the treehouse. He cleared a path through the slippery needles on the ground and laid stones in at regular intervals, creating a terraced walkway that could endure winter rain. He bought the wood and nails and cement as promised, but he also picked up a big bucket of green paint on clearance and a little four-pane window and frame. The door would be made out of a chunk of paneled fencing from the hardware store's scrap pile.

Max did most of the work, but Penny helped by hoisting materials and tools up to him on a winch once the floor was laid and the walls started going up. When they were done, father and daughter stood and admired the new construction with their hands stuck in their back pockets.

"I'm lucky my dad's so good at making itty-bitty houses," Penny said, grinning.

"Yep. Although this is the biggest one I've made in a long while." Max dug around in his toolbox, and handed Penny a paintbrush. "All right, I did all the hard stuff. I still need to tighten the screws on the roof, but it'll only take a few minutes. There's no reason you can't start painting now. Just be careful on the ladder, it's sort of tacked on at the moment."

Unlike their new home, the treehouse would have a slanted roof. Max wondered if he could give the big house the same treatment. He wasn't looking forward to scraping puddles and moss off the flat roof every month or two. That kind of construction would be too big a job for him to handle alone, though. He'd have to hire a contractor.

Copper mewed. The kitten was sitting next to a neighboring tree, secured into a tiny red harness that was tied to a branch. In the first four days of wearing it, he had screamed like a banshee and clawed at everything in sight, but Penny had stuck to her guns and he was finally getting used to it.

"Almost done, Copper," Penny said. "Just have to paint now, and then we can have a tea party. Oh!"

"What? What's wrong?"

"Nothing! I just found this. Thanks, Dad! It's so cute!"

"What?"

Penny held out a brass door knocker in the shape of a cat's head. The cat held a loop in its teeth, which could be knocked against an attached piece of metal shaped like a paw.

"I love it!" Penny said, holding it up to the little door to see how it would look. "How should we attach it?"

Max stared. "I uh…I didn't buy that, hon. Where did you find it?"

"Very funny, Dad. It was right here on the floor, and you know it."

Max nodded. His lips were numb. "Sure, right. Well, it doesn't have any holes tapped in it, so we'll have to just glue it on."

His mind raced. Had Emily played a trick on them? Maybe it was that weird fellow from the contest, Puck. He couldn't think of a single reason for the appearance of the gift that didn't sound like trouble. But he didn't have the heart to take the door knocker away from Penny, no matter where it came from. It was perfect—a final touch that was exactly what the treehouse needed to look complete.

After the roof was installed and the ladder permanently secured to the door frame, Max and Penny sat on the porch and ate dinner in view of the treehouse. From their seats they stared at their creation from time to time, admiring it, basking in the satisfaction of a job well done. Penny's cheeks were smeared with green paint, and Max's fingers were sticky with glue.

"It's amazing," Penny whispered, setting her fork down on her plate. When she looked up at Max, her eyes were watery. "Thanks, Dad. For everything."

"You're welcome, kid. I love you."

"Love you too."

CHAPTER 7

As Max had anticipated, Penny's excitement at her early parole from the school year soon withered into boredom. Without friends nearby, she struggled to fill her afternoons. Her homework sessions moved earlier and earlier in the day, until she was getting out of bed almost as early as she had in the fall. Afternoons were spent training Copper, nagging Max, and painting the inside of the green treehouse with a thousand little pictures: flowers, stars, fish, birds, and rainbows.

Working from home meant Max made his own schedule. Often, that also meant forgetting to take time off, so he had a strict rule about not working on Sundays—not out of any particular religious tradition, but just so he wouldn't work a month straight without thinking about it and wind up wondering why he felt so tired all the time.

One particular Sunday in mid-May, he devoted the whole day to baking. Penny would not be recruited; nothing in the whole world was more boring than baking, she said. Max turned out two dozen cookies, a dozen miniature meat pies cooked in a muffin tin, a loaf of spice bread, and thirty-four rosemary butter biscuits. There had been thirty-six, but two were lost to the floor and had ended up in Copper's tummy.

By four o'clock, Max realized he hadn't seen Penny in hours. She had taken to spending late afternoons in the treehouse, so he loaded a paper plate with cookies and fruit and made his way up the slope, with the food draped under a towel to keep the bugs away.

"Madame," he called out from the bottom of the ladder in his snootiest voice. "Your maitre d' has arrived with her majesty's afternoon snack."

Penny poked her head out the door. "That's not what a maitre d' does."

"Ah. I see. Well, then I guess these cookies will need to be disposed of in some other way, then." Max fished a cookie out from under the towel and stuffed it in his mouth.

"Umm…maybe I'm wrong about that, after all." Penny grinned. "Those look pretty good. Give me a minute, and I'll come down."

"No need. I'll bring them up." Max passed the plate from one hand to the other before he realized, to his dismay, he could not climb the ladder one-handed. He folded the plate in half and gripped it in his teeth.

"Dad, that's a terrible idea."

His jaw ached by the time he reached the treehouse door, but he made it. Penny had been right; it was a terrible idea. But he had succeeded without falling and making an ass out of himself, so he didn't feel he had to admit his mistake.

"I don't think we'll both fit inside, so I'll just leave these here," he said, winking from the ladder. "Wow. You've really done a lot of work on the walls. Looks great!"

Some of the drawings were done in crayon, but many were painted with the leftover colors from a paint-by-number Penny's mother had sent her last Christmas. Cats and birds played as friends under rainbows of different palettes; pastel, bold, black and grey, striped and spotted. Green vines twisted and wound their way through the creatures and shapes, joining up with the rainbows before exploding into fireworks made of leaves and flower petals.

"Thanks. I'm just bored, I guess," Penny said.

"Nonsense. This is beautiful, and really creative. Guess you take after me, huh?"

Penny shrugged. "Or maybe you take after me."

"That's not how it…" A large drawing in the center
of the opposite wall caught Max's eye. It sent chills up his
back and numbed his hands, loosening his grip on the
ladder's top rung. "Penny? What's that?"

"What? Oh, the wapiti? I saw one out in the woods a
few days ago, so I added it to the mural."

"A what?"

"A wapiti. An elk."

"Where'd you learn that word?"

"It's Shawnee. You know, Native American. I learned it
from my homework for my American history class."

Max's body had started to complain about clinging to
the ladder, but he couldn't tear his eyes away from the animal's intense gaze. If it was the same giant elk he had seen
the week before, Penny had drawn it just right; its rack of
antlers spread wide on either side of its head—although
she had covered them in little flowers—and its eyes were a
liquid black-red with pupils shaped like diamonds.

"Why didn't you tell me?"

"About what?"

"The elk. I saw one too, and it was huge. You never
mentioned seeing one."

"I forgot," Penny shrugged.

"You forgot you saw a sixteen-foot tall elk?"

"It was just a big moose, Dad. There's lots of wildlife
out here."

"Not a moose. An elk."

"Same thing."

"No, it's…"

But Max's shoulders were about to give out. He
climbed down the ladder, escaping the painted elk's cold
stare. He chided himself for the wave of relief he felt once
he was below its sight-line. Why had a child's drawing

made him feel so nervous?

"Come in for dinner soon, okay?" he called up to Penny.

"Mmhm," she said around a mouthful of cookie.

Max examined the forest. There was no movement now, no sign of the elk. But some of the trees were scraped high in their branches, about sixteen feet up. The bark had been rubbed off until the raw fleshy wood underneath was exposed bare.

The Yellow Pages had several listings for deer fence installation. Max thumbed through the ads, feeling out of his depth; he'd never before had to worry about a wild animal bigger than a mouse. He settled on a small company that was a father-and-son business, and was available to do the work within the week.

Maybe he was being paranoid. He didn't know anything about elk. The creature was probably harmless, and it wasn't like Max had a garden to protect. But something about the animal was unsettling, and he didn't want it getting anywhere near Penny or Copper.

On the day of the fence installation, a battered white truck backed all the way around the circular driveway until the tailgate was pointed at the side of the house. Russel, the man he'd spoken to on the phone, shook Max's hand with a tattered glove and pointed over his shoulder with a thumb at his son, Jerry. The younger man was in his twenties and had a crop of bright red hair, inexpertly trimmed.

"I'm Russel, and that's Jerry. Nice to meet you, Mr. Braun. We're ready to get started, just as soon as you point the way."

"You can follow the blue ribbons," Max said. "They're tied to trees marking the whole perimeter, about ten feet apart. Can't miss them."

"You want us to create a break anywhere? Might be nice to have a gate so you can get past the fence without going all the way around."

Max thought about it. "Would that make the fence any weaker? We have some pretty big wildlife out here."

Russel shook his head. "Shouldn't."

Max frowned. "Know what? Don't worry about it. Just keep it solid. The property behind isn't mine, so I shouldn't be going out there anyway."

"All right then."

Max watched them unload metal poles and netting from their truck, then directed them to a clearing at the side of the house where the materials could be stored. Penny peeked out the window once, made a bored face, and went back to her homework.

"How long do you think the job will take?" Max asked.

"Five days, probably, unless we run into any big issues. We'll have to cut a few trees down, and that's what takes the most time. After that we'll just need to dig some holes and plant some poles." Russel smiled, showing a few holes of his own; many of his teeth were missing, and some of the rest were only half there.

Around noon, Max took a walk across the property. He knocked the needles off the roof of the treehouse and watered the potted plants on the front porch, but he was mostly checking to see if the father-and-son outfit were still hard at work. They were, and had made good progress; two small trees had been removed, ten poles were already drying in their cement anchors, and the netting was unrolled nearby. He left them to their labor and made his way toward the mailbox at the street.

Mr. Samson, the venerable USPS foot-soldier, was

passing by.

"Samson! Any mail in your bag for us yet?"

"No, sir. Guess the post office still hasn't caught up with your address change."

"Damn. I'll have to head over to the branch myself, see what's going on."

"Won't do no good," Mr. Samson muttered.

"What was that?"

Mr. Samson shook his head, but the workmen's white truck caught his eye. He frowned with confusion, then with alarm. "You got workers here?"

"Yeah, installing a wildlife fence. You wouldn't believe the size of the deer I saw a couple weeks ago. It…"

"A fence? Here?"

"Well, yes. To keep the wildlife out. As I said."

Mr. Samson turned his face toward Max with an expression he found indecipherable. It seemed a mix of fear, confusion, and dismay.

"It's letting you?"

"What's letting me? What are you talking about?"

Mr. Samson put his head down, clutched his mail bag, and continued his route down the street without another word. Max watched him with his hands on his hips, shaking his head. What a weird old bird.

From the forest near the house came a scream. It was short and shocked; a wet, high sound, filled with acidic terror.

Another yell came from the forest, this one deeper. Then there was a crash.

Max sprinted up the hill, and Mr. Samson sprinted away down the street as fast as his old legs could carry him.

By the time Max reached the worksite, both father and son were dead. A thirty-foot pine tree had uprooted and toppled over on the father. Only one leg and one arm were visible under the massive trunk. Blood had splattered in every direction in a red explosion shaped like a child's drawing of a sun, long arms of liquid shot across the needle-coated ground. The tree bark was damaged halfway up its trunk, fresh wounds scraped open by the antlers of a large animal.

The younger of the two men was not whole. His torso was separated at the belt line; chunks of tree bark stuck to his shirt, as if his body had been used like an axe against the pine. His lower half was nowhere to be seen.

A large red lump that must have been the rest of the father lay nearby, pulped into an unrecognizable mass. Sticks and splintered bone poked out from the mound of flesh, which was seeping into a pile of fresh mulch. Then Max understood; the man had somehow been caught up in his wood chipper.

"Dad?" Penny called from her bedroom window. "What's going on?"

"Stay inside!" Max yelled, frightened at the tinny screech he heard in his own voice. "Don't come out here! Call an ambulance. There's been an…" Max swallowed. An accident? Was that what it was, really?

The ground around the worksite had been trampled flat by a thousand teardrop-shaped prints. They were in pairs, like a flurry of quotation marks. Max wasn't sure he had ever seen elk hooves before in his life, yet he had no doubt about the origin of those tracks.

And what would he tell the police when they arrived? The carnage didn't look like the work of a man, but it was brutal, horrific. Max turned his back on the scene, unable to look without feeling bile rising in his throat. Even if the deaths weren't his fault, they were his problem. The yard would soon be crawling with cops if he called it in. They would bring ambulances, but the workmen were beyond the help of any doctor, so what was the point of that? The press would show up, first the local, and then maybe national. And then the men's next of kin would be called. Max might be sued. His insurance company might even be contacted. He'd lose work, lose clients. Lawyers and adjusters and reporters and…

He could lose the house.

"Penny!" he called, hating himself. "Meet me in the kitchen. We need to talk."

Max sat across from his daughter at the dinner table, trying not to show the depth of his shock. He kept his shaking hands clasped in his lap, except for when he took a sip from his glass.

He could tell Penny understood what he was telling her and didn't fully believe his story. She was a smart kid, and his lies were flimsy. But whether he told Penny the truth or not, those men would stay dead. Nothing could change that now. And the only people who had anything to lose by involving the authorities were Max and Penny.

"What about their truck?" Penny said. "It's still sitting outside."

Max winced. He had forgotten about the truck. It was bad enough he was lying to her about what had happened to the men, but now he had to add to his pile of untruths. "They left without it. An ambulance picked them both up, and they said they'd come back for the truck in a couple of days. After they get out of the hospital."

"An ambulance came already? That was fast. And I didn't hear a siren."

"Well, I called right away. And an ambulance was already in the area. The important thing is that we don't tell anyone else there was an accident, understand? That's what you need to remember. We have to protect ourselves from people who might pry. People like your mother."

Penny nodded, scrunching up her face, trying not to cry. She knew her mother was untrustworthy, and that understanding hurt her. Max's self-hatred deepened.

"Well, the emergency nurses told me they're both going to be fine, so we can stop worrying about it. A tree fell, that's all. It happens all the time. Tomorrow, I'll just pick up where they left off, since all the supplies are still out there."

"You're still going to finish the fence? But…"

"We need the fence. We have to protect our property. But I don't want anyone else back there until it's done, and that includes you. Wait until I say it's okay."

"Dad, I'm scared. Something feels really wrong. Like it's not safe here. Maybe we should just move away."

Max's heart sank. Never! He'd never leave this house; it was a miracle they were here at all. How could he make her understand that? She was just a kid, with no idea how the real world worked. No idea what a dollar was worth, or what a real house meant to a family.

She also had no idea that the elk was responsible for the disappearance of the workmen. A tree had fallen, there had been an accident, that was all. Max didn't mention the animal to her, and she didn't need to know; it would only make her more frightened.

"That's enough for now. I need to go take care of the back yard. Don't look outside again until I say it's safe, okay? I don't want you to see. Like I said, the men were badly injured. So it's pretty gross out there. But everything's going to be fine. I promise."

Penny nodded, and carried Copper down the hall without looking toward the back yard. After closing her door, Max heard a tiny "click." For the first time in her life, she had locked herself in her room.

Max located the son's lower half hanging from a branch
he could only reach by standing on top of the treehouse
and poking at it with a broomstick until it fell to the
ground with a queasy thud. He buried the remains of the
men just outside his property line, shoveling every little
bit of blood-soaked dirt and every red needle into the
graves along with the bodies. The forest floor around the
fence-building site was scraped clean when he was done.
After the graves were filled in, the largest outstanding fac-
tor was the truck. But he knew just what to do with that.

    He hadn't driven up Skyline Drive since the day they
moved out of the old apartment. It was three o'clock in
the morning when he arrived at the top curve, and traffic
was light. He waited until a car had just passed, and no
headlights were making the winding drive up the hillside.
Then he put the truck in neutral, released the brake, and
rolled it off the edge. It missed the first line of trees, just as
he'd hoped it would. Obvious damage to the outer trunks
might lead someone to investigate. But it passed safely between two old pines, and smashed further down. He didn't
think the truck would be visible from the street, even in
the daylight.

    It was done. All evidence of the incident had been
hidden, and no one else knew about it…

    Max froze, remembering. No. Someone else did know.
Mr. Samson, the mailman, had also heard the screams. Mr.
Samson had been right there outside the house when it
happened.

    He wanted to run, to find the man, to explain what
had happened, tell any lie he had to…but even if that had
been an option, Max was stuck on Skyline Drive without a
car. He needed to find a payphone to call a taxi before he

could even begin to head home. His heart pounded in his chest as he considered his options. Maybe he could pay the man off, if he hadn't said anything to anyone yet. But what were the chances of that?

Max sat by his mailbox the next day, waiting for the letters that never came. Mr. Samson was running late. It seemed likely he wouldn't show up at all, given the terror Max had seen in the man's eyes before he had sprinted down the street.

But he did arrive, plodding down the street in his usual manner. He nodded at Max as if everything was perfectly normal, and continued on his route without a second glance.

"Mr. Samson? Wait. Can we talk?"

The mail carrier stopped and put his head down, shaking it at the asphalt without turning back toward Max. "Don't wanna talk about it. Don't wanna know. None of my business."

"But you heard the accident, I know you did. Let me explain what happened…"

"No need. Don't bother. Not your fault, whatever it was."

"Um…"

Mr. Samson looked up, and turned his head to glare at the trees behind the house. Max could only see half of the man's face, but recognized the fear that still lingered there.

"You be careful with your little girl, that's all. This place is dangerous, always has been, somehow. Don't know why, don't want to know. And if you do know why, don't tell me. You leave me alone, and I'll leave you alone. That's all."

Max was dumbfounded, but let the little man truck along, lugging his bag of letters with him. When he turned back toward the house, he felt chills run up his arms, making the hairs stand at attention. For the first time, he noticed the front windows looked like staring eyes. He was being judged, and found guilty. Not of murder, of course not. But of disrespect to a corpse, certainly. And, far worse, of recruiting his daughter into his deceit.

As he walked up the curving driveway towards the house, a breeze picked up, carrying with it the scent of an old fire. And Max's mouth tasted of ashes.

CHAPTER 8

As soon as the fence was installed, Max found the peace of mind he had been seeking. His castle was secure, his daughter was safe, and new work was rolling in. A wealthy hobbyist in Vancouver wanted half a town built; library, city hall, drive-in theater, elementary school, public pool. It would keep Max busy for weeks. He buried himself in his work to forget what was buried on the hillside.

Penny continued to paint the treehouse. Over the picture of the elk, she painted a big black rose with a smaller red rose at its center. When every inch of the inside walls was crowded with drawings, she started on the exterior, balancing atop a metal ladder. Watching her stand on her toes ten feet above the ground made Max jittery, but he left her alone. Her cheeks flushed with excitement when she painted, a blossoming artist just discovering her own unique talents. He didn't have the heart to stop her. Instead, he bought more paint and a new set of brushes, and laid every blanket and towel from the house on the ground under where she was working to cushion her fall in case she ever lost her balance. Copper decided the padding was as good as a bed, and kept watch underneath. He came into the house every evening for dinner with a rainbow of paint drops speckling his orange fur.

When Max finished the Vancouver job, he was left with that hollow, lost-in-the-woods feeling he always had after completing a major project. He had packaged each little building up in shipping paper, written a personal note to the buyer, and left the miniature masterpieces in the dubious care of the United States Postal Service. Summer was just getting started, which always signaled a

slowdown in business. Winter was the time for huddling
in basements, working on miniatures, building train set
props for Christmas or perfect replicas of peoples' homes
and families for Valentine's Day. But when the first heat
wave hit, everyone rushed outdoors and stopped placing
orders. Max had saved up enough for groceries for the
next few months, but he would need to find something
else to do with his time until at least September, maybe
even October.

He wandered over to Penny's treehouse a few times
a day, bugging her as much as she had bugged him the
previous month. As he watched, day after day, a tangle
of painted vines sprouted from the windowsills, poppies
bloomed in bright rows, and a constellation of white stars
appeared on a dark purple sky that started under the treehouse's eaves and continued up over the peak of its roof.
Gnomes marched in a line along the wall that faced the
main house, and elves danced on high-wire ropes, holding
lollipops and pinwheels in their little pink hands.

"This is really something, Penny," Max said. He meant
it. The drawings were amateur but effective. She was showing real skill. How much did art college tuition cost these
days?

"Thanks, Dad. Do you think I have room for a unicorn?"

"There's always room for a unicorn. Although it might
have to be a small one."

"Hmm." Penny chose a spot on the corner closest to
the woods. "I'll put it over here, so it can protect us."

"Well, that's what the fence is for."

Penny glanced down at her father with a withering,
aged look. For a moment, she seemed much older than
eleven. It was the first time Max could recollect her re-
garding him with pity, or perhaps even condescension.

"Dad, if you don't mind—and please don't take this personally—but could you come back later? I just need to focus."

"Oh! No problem, kid. I have some stuff to do anyway." Max jammed his hands in his pockets and lumbered back toward the house.

Damn, she was growing up fast. A little over a year from now, she'd be a teenager. He wasn't ready for that, and he knew it.

Max bumbled around the house, feeling ancient. Everything was clean. Everything was cooked. He checked the mailbox again; still nothing there. When he was at the post office with the package for Vancouver, he had inquired about any backed up letters or bills. They had insisted there were none. What else could he do? The electricity hadn't been turned off, and the water was still flowing through the taps. If a utility company had a problem with nonpayment, or they sent a bill collector to his door, he'd worry about it then. The whole thing would sort itself out, eventually.

Max put his hands on his lower back and leaned left, right, forward, back. Pop-pop-pop. He touched his toes— well, almost. When he came up short he reached harder, until his back sent him a warning twinge and he laid off the calisthenics.

A thin stripe of purple caught his eye. It was a beautiful, royal color, barely visible in a thin line on the wall above the living room carpet. Like a string of festive yarn along the bottom of the wall's otherwise modern cheese-cake-colored plaster. Crawling on his hands and knees, he pressed his fingers on the carpet where it touched the walls and found more of the color; it extended down to the floor. Sloppy paint job, most likely. He could probably match the cream color with a mix of paint from his workshop—but the purple called to him. It was interesting.

He sat back on his heels and frowned at the carpet. It had never been much to his liking. He pried back a corner, yanking the tiny tacks from the trim under the wall, and found some nice wooden boards underneath. They were very much like the ones that held up the house's odd, flat roof. A hardwood floor would really add a lot to the mood of the place. Not as warm, maybe, but the idea of making the house feel more like a mountain cabin was appealing.

Yanking at the carpet revealed more wood. It needed staining and had some minor water damage, but it was generally in good condition and appeared to be less than ten years old. Max was unable to peel up the carpet past the spot where the television console sat, but he had seen enough to decide it was worth renovating. It was just the right kind of project for him to spend his summer on. He'd need some new tools, a sander, and a larger amount of wood stain than he usually kept on hand.

A thin line of green caught his eye. Max leaned forward until his nose nearly touched the wood. There, in a crack between the boards, was a pine needle. Not just one, in fact, but the entire gap was filled with them. He dug a few out with his fingernail, and noticed that every crack between every board was filled with the needles, as if the floor had been exposed to the forest for a long time. How was that possible?

The phone rang, and Max yelped in surprise. Struggling to his feet—oh, how his knees ached now, he was too old to crouch like that for long—his back popped again. He groaned in pain and let out a little fart. Good thing Penny was outside; his ego couldn't take any more of her pity today.

He fumbled the phone receiver to his ear. "Max here." Why had he said that? That wasn't how he normally answered the phone. It was just one of those days, apparently.

"Max! Great to hear your voice again! Walter Puck, Elkstone Giveaways. Haven't spoken to you in six weeks or so, thought I'd check in, see how things are going in the new house!"

"Well things are just fine here," Max said. His voice cracked, and he cleared his throat. "Just fine. We love it. Built a treehouse for Penny, and she's painting it herself right now. She's in hog heaven."

"Wow! That sounds fantastic. Fantastic. I just wanted to reach out and let you know about a special offer we have going on here at the office today. We're having a big sale on time!"

"Time?"

"That's right! Months, years, even decades. A little for you, and a ton for your daughter! For a low, low price, you can have a whole lot more *time*."

"I don't understand."

"Let me be a little more clear then. If you want to continue to live, keep your fucking hands off the house. Put the carpet back, forget what you saw underneath it, and get along back to your wonderful life! This is a one-time special, good for today only. If you decide to pass on our offer, I'll never mention it again. I give you my word. Although I wouldn't need to, because you'd be all out of time. And so would your beautiful daughter! So, what do you think? Do we have a deal?"

Max coughed into the phone. When he was able to speak again, his voice was a harsh whisper. "Deal."

The line went dead.

Max sat in the new modern lounge chair he had bought to replace his beloved corduroy recliner. He thought now of that battered old beast with deep, aching longing. It was more than nostalgia. That ugly brown thing had been the most comfortable chair in the world, and he had betrayed it. Sent it off to slaughter on a whim, under the pretense of starting fresh. And what was the point of that?

The phone call had ended an hour ago, but his hands were still shaking. Another stress test for his heart; still good, still ticking along. His mind was another matter. Thoughts raced to and fro, trying to make connections between pieces of information that had none. A floor that looked like a roof. A roof that looked like a floor. Pine needles and purple paint. Elkstone. Elk. But the Shawnee called them wapiti.

Penny screamed. Max blinked and was outside; his reflexes had lifted him from his chair and shot him halfway across the yard before his eyes could focus in the daylight.

"Penny!" he howled. "Penny, where are you? What's wrong?"

He slipped on dead needles, landed hard on his knee on one of the cobblestone steps, and was up again before he had time to curse about it.

Penny was clinging to the ladder, unharmed. She pointed at the bit of fencing that was visible where it emerged from the forest, her mouth wide open with shock. Max followed her line of sight and saw the fence had been uprooted, the metal poles warped. He hadn't heard it happen, but it hadn't been like that earlier that afternoon. Whoever had trashed the fence had managed to do so without making a sound.

Out of the woods emerged the largest hare Max had ever seen. It was black with a white tufted tail, streaked with blood. And it was watching them with glowing red eyes.

"Inside the house, Penny! Now!"

Penny climbed down the ladder faster than was safe,

and as soon as her sneakers hit the dirt Max grabbed her arm, pulling her along with him in a manner he hadn't done since the time when she was a toddler and almost fell into the community pool. She tripped over her own feet behind him but he pressed on, dragging her toward the house. By the time the sliding door was shut and locked, the hare had disappeared into the forest.

"Just what the hell is going on with the wildlife around here?" Max said, breathing hard. "Why are all the animals so messed up?"

"It was the same one, Dad. The hare and the elk are the same…*thing*, somehow."

"How do you know that?"

Penny looked through the glass, her gaze fixated on the hillside pines. "I was painting bunnies when he showed up."

"So?"

She shook her head. "I don't know how I know. But it was the wapiti. Just wearing a different set of clothes."

"What happened to the fence? Did you see?"

Penny shook her head, then her eyes went glassy. Max caught her as she slid to the floor in a faint. Seconds later, she woke up halfway and asked for water. Not wanting to leave her alone, he carried her to the kitchen table and sat her in a chair before taking a glass from the cupboard.

"He talked to me," she said.

"What? Who?"

"A few days ago. In the treehouse, before I painted over his face. He told me his name."

"The elk?"

"I don't remember what he said, though. I'm so sorry, Dad."

"You have nothing to be sorry about, Penny. What else do you remember?"

Penny closed her eyes and leaned forward, drifting into sleep. Max wondered if he should keep her awake, and decided not to. When he put her to bed, he rested his hand on her forehead. It was hot. Not burning up, but she probably had a mild fever.

He sat by her bed for hours, keeping the water glass ready, watching her sleep. As the room darkened into evening, he thought about the house, the hare, and Walter Puck. Max was a staunch atheist, but he'd have to be delusional to pretend everything was normal here. Nothing he had seen in his forty-two mundane years could explain away the unnatural events that had occurred over the last month. The way he saw it, he had two choices; he could run away, or fight. If he ran away, he would be homeless. And that meant he would lose Penny.

There was only one answer, then. The house was his, and Penny was his. And he would do whatever it took to keep both.

CHAPTER 9

Max held the phone receiver away from his ear as Emily bawled. She stopped every couple minutes to blow snot from her nose with two short blasts—honk, honk—and sniff up the rest, long and hard. In their years of marriage, Max had never had the heart to tell her she sounded exactly like an angry goose whenever she cried. First the honking, then the hissing.

"Slow down, Em. Tell me again what happened."

"Took…took all my money. Ran off with Rebecca, that bitch from Hawaii. He took my car, too. Must have stolen the keys right out of my purse. Oh, god, I'm so stupid…" she tapered off again, then dissolved into another crying jag.

Max resented the blossoming, warm satisfaction he felt growing from his toes to his nose. Sure, she deserved what she got. But he didn't want to be the type of person who gloats over another's misfortune. Anyway, he and Emily had enjoyed a few good years of marriage. And they had Penny together, of course. That counted for an awful lot.

"You gonna be okay? You have any savings to tide you over?"

"I did, but he got it all. Just walked right into the bank…I think he must have been a pro, Max. What am I going to do? Oh, god."

Max struggled. His head told him she was nothing but trouble, but his heart wanted to invite her into his home. He had no way of knowing how clean she was, but he wanted to believe she wouldn't use drugs around Penny.

Anyway, how safe was the house, really? He hadn't

heard from Walter Puck for two weeks, but that didn't
mean much. More sections of the deer fence had been
uprooted every couple of days, and Max had just let the
whole thing go. Penny played in her treehouse only under
Max's supervision. Emily would wonder about that, and
what would he say? That a creature which was alternately
an elk and a hare and a telephone contest host had torn up
their fence and murdered two men?

"Look, I have some extra cash," Max said. It was a lie.
It wasn't extra, and he couldn't afford to lend it, but he was
a sucker. "Let me swing by, drop it off. Tomorrow afternoon okay?"

"Max, I can't…"

"You can, and you will. It's fine. I've had a run of luck
lately." Another lie.

"Bring Penny with you? If she wants to, I mean."

Max frowned at the phone. His money wasn't enough
for her? She had to make this even harder? But that wasn't
fair; Penny was her daughter, too.

"All right. If she wants to. But if she doesn't, I'm not
making her."

Emily again sobbed softly, this time with gratitude.
"Of course. I understand. Thank you, Max."

Penny flatly refused to go with Max, but he talked her into
writing her mother a nice letter. Just a casual note, with
a few updates on the treehouse and Copper. These days,
Penny seemed a little afraid of her mother. And was that
so surprising? Before the separation, sometimes it was
hard to tell whether it was Emily or the drugs doing the
talking. Penny wasn't ready to forgive her mother, wasn't
even ready to see her again. But she wrote the letter, and
Max tucked it into his shirt pocket with pride.

"You did good, Penny. I know you don't want to see

her, and that's fine. But she's going to love this letter."

Penny shrugged. She was acting more like a teenager every day. Father-daughter talks had become less frequent; most of her time was spent drawing and painting, sleeping next to Copper, and eating everything in the house. Max hoped when school started she would normalize a little. He had tried to organize a playdate with one of her old friends, and was surprised when Penny refused the offer without giving him any reason why.

"You absolutely sure you don't want to see her today?"

"Yeah. I'm sure."

"Okay. It's up to you. But you can't stay here alone. I'll be gone for at least five hours. I'm going to drop you off at the Roseville library."

"But Dad!"

"No way. If you want to call one of your friends to see if they can meet you there, go ahead and do it now. But you're not staying here without me, especially for that long."

Penny scowled, and picked up the phone. She stared at it as if she had forgotten how to use it.

"I forgot everyone's number." Her annoyance turned to worry. "Dad, I forgot everyone! It's like they don't even exist anymore."

"That's silly, Penny. Look in the address book. I probably have most of their numbers in there on the PTA meeting roster."

Penny found not one, but three friends eager to meet her at the library. When Max dropped her off at the front steps, her hair was gathered in a single ponytail at the back of her head instead of the pigtails she used to favor. As she slammed the car door and ran up toward the lobby entrance, he could swear she had grown an inch taller since yesterday. She turned and waved before going inside, smiling with relief in the familiar surroundings.

Max drove off grinning. It was just what the kid needed, and he'd figured that out just by instinct alone, even
against her own protestations. Ladies and gentlemen, may
I present Mr. Maxwell Braun: Father of the Year.

Emily had dried up in the two hours since the phone call.
Her eyes were still red and her makeup had been washed
away, but she had stopped sniffling and honking her nose.
She met him in the apartment complex driveway and
hopped into his car without an invitation, thanking him
while taking advantage of him without missing a beat.
That was Emily.

"I'm so glad to see you, Max. Really. I don't know
what I'm going to do. He took it all, Max, every last cent!
I'd been saving up, and he just ran off with it. I can't believe
I got conned. Could we do one thing real quick? I just
need to go to the store…"

"Where'd you meet this guy, Emily?"

"Hmm?"

"Your boyfriend. The one who ran off with your
money, remember him?" Max hated the sarcasm he heard
in his voice, and tried to tone it down. "Where'd you meet
him?"

"Oh, just at a bar. He was a bartender. Or at least that's
what he told me. God knows what he really…"

"At a bar? Or out back in the alley behind the bar?"

Emily put her face in her hands. "Fine. Yes, Max. I
know what you're asking. If it makes you feel better, you're
right. He was a dealer, okay? You win."

"It doesn't make me feel better. But if I'm going to take
a five-hour round trip to drop money off at your doorstep, I want to know what the situation is. Will he retaliate
against me for helping you? Do we need to worry about

Penny's safety? That's what I want to know."

Emily shook her head. "It's not like that. He's not a big deal, no connections or anything. Just a regular user with a side hustle. And, apparently, a side piece." Emily frowned out the window, gazing up at her apartment building.

Her grief seemed genuine to Max. He couldn't know for sure if she was grieving the loss of her partner or the loss of her money, but he decided not to withhold help either way. From his shirt pocket he pulled an envelope full of twenties, along with the folded paper that was Penny's dutiful note for her mother.

"What's…" Emily started, before unfolding the paper. "Oh my god. I didn't think she'd…"

"She didn't want to see you, but she wrote that for you. It's something, at least."

Emily's tears started anew. "I can't thank you enough, Max. I know you told her to write this, but just…thank you."

"I didn't make her write it. I only suggested it. She was the one who decided."

Emily blew her nose. Honk, honk. Sniff.

A car pulled up behind Max and beeped. He was blocking the driveway.

"Look, Emily, have you eaten? Can I take you to lunch?"

"Oh, I can't…"

"Well I need to move or this guy behind me is going to have a conniption fit. Yes or no?"

"Yes."

Max pulled the car around and headed toward Ronnie's Diner, a greasy little pit stop off the northbound interstate. Back when he and Emily were married, their go-to spot was Big Don's, which was right next door and served the best hamburgers in the state. Too many memories in that joint, though. That shark-infested water was too deep to tread today.

Emily ordered a salad—with lobster, of course—and Max settled for a bowl of vegetable soup. The strangeness of the day had robbed him of his appetite, and he was also becoming increasingly conscious of his overall health. If life was going to keep throwing curveballs, he wanted to make sure he was ready to dodge.

Emily picked at her fifteen-dollar salad, and wiped at her wet eyes with a paper napkin. "Max, do you ever think about us?"

"Us?"

"You know. Maybe trying again. I know I've made a lot of mistakes, but I'm clean now. And I think I miss you."

"You think?"

Emily reached out and rested her hand on Max's. "More than think. I'm sure of it. I miss you and Penny, and I want to see you both more often. I still can't drive, of course. They won't give me back my license because of the Skyline accident. But if we really want to, we can find a way, I know we can."

Max withdrew his hand from the table top. "How long have you been clean? I mean really, really clean."

"Six weeks, three days, eight hours."

Max nodded. "Good start. Let's give it a little longer." He sipped his soup, but watched her reaction. What she did next would tell him more about her progress than her words ever could. The old Emily would fly into a rage, shout at him, make selfish demands.

Emily swallowed hard. She stared at the table, blinked back tears, and forced a big bite of lobster salad. Max nodded.

"Penny's not ready yet, Emily," he said. "If she was, she'd be here with me now. I care more about her than I do about myself, or about rekindling our relationship. But when she's ready, we'll talk about this again. I promise. Okay?"

Emily beamed. "Yes. Thank you, Max."

By the time lunch was over, Emily was dried up again. Max drove her home, and before she opened the passenger door she leaned over and kissed his cheek. It was an unexpected, tender act. He looked into her eyes and found nothing there but loneliness and pleading and pain. Answering her request for comfort, he placed a gentle hand behind her head and pressed his lips against hers. She melted against him, put her hand on his knee, and shuddered.

Max pulled back. "I have to go. Penny's waiting for me to pick her up."

Emily nodded. After he pulled the car away from the curb, he looked in the rear view mirror to find her watching him drive away. She held Penny's letter to her chest, and her tears were streaming again.

Penny was sitting on the library steps when he pulled up. Her hair had come out of its ponytail and she was laughing, red-cheeked, along with two giddy girlfriends. The cold nervousness of the last two months was gone, replaced by her usual enthusiasm. Max sighed with relief; there was his little girl. He felt more strongly now than ever that she would be fine once school started up again.

Penny skipped toward the car, waving back at her friends.

"Have fun?" Max asked.

"Yeah! It was great. Bonnie got a boyfriend! And Heather went to summer camp, but she came back early because her aunt died, and…"

"You know, if you want to see them again, I'll drive

you."

"Dad! It's hours away!"

Max nodded. "Yep. But it's important. If you want to see them again next weekend, you arrange it and I'll drive you, okay?"

"Really? You sure?"

"Of course I'm sure."

Penny grinned. "Okay. Um…how's Mom?"

"She's all right. A little sad, but she'll be fine. And she loved your letter."

"Hmm." Penny stared out the window.

Two hours later, Max pulled the car into the long, circular driveway. The summer sun was still out, just visible over the pine tree tops. A squadron of wrens fluttered up from the front yard as the car approached the front door, and a raccoon which had been rooting in the trash can scuttled away toward the trees.

"It's been a while, hasn't it?" Penny said. "Since we saw him."

"Saw who?" Max asked, knowing well who she meant.

"The one with the red diamond eyes."

"I don't think you should call it 'him,' Penny. It's just a weird animal."

She turned to glare at him as he cut the ignition. "Why are you lying to me?"

Max started, "I'd never…" but stopped. She was right. "Okay, yes. I admit, it's something more than an animal. But I think we should avoid talking about it. We've been doing fine so far, haven't we?"

Penny locked the car door. "I have to tell you something, Dad. I should have told you before."

Max's blood ran cold. "What is it? You know you can tell me anything you want."

Penny started to cry. When the tears ran down her face, she looked like her mother. "He came to me a couple times. As the hare, not the elk. Right up to my window. He talked to me. Not with his mouth…he can't really talk, he's just a weird bunny. But I heard his voice in my mind."

"When?" Max's mouth was dry. His heart thumped against his breastbone.

"Last week, and again last night. He told me the house was his. He told me…" Penny sobbed. "That I was his."

A pulsing red tidal wave of anger flooded Max's vision. *His!* Penny was his daughter! His hands made fists. "He said that? You know that isn't true. It will never be true."

"He was looking in my room, Dad…"

Max's paternal rage insisted he punch something, and he aimed for the driver's side door. The panel popped in and back out again. The sound made Penny jump, and self-loathing overlapped the anger in Max's heart.

"I'm sorry, I'm so sorry. I didn't mean to scare you. He's just a ghost, Penny. At least, I think he's a ghost. I don't think he'll hurt us. Maybe he just wants us to move out of the house."

Penny nodded. "I think so too. He didn't hurt me. But it's scary, Dad. I still think we should move away. Maybe we can…"

"No!" Max yelled, scaring her again. She turned to him with wide, bloodshot eyes. "Sorry. I'm sorry I shouted, but we can't leave. We have to fight for this house, Penny. It's our house, and if we have to fight to stay, then that's what we'll do. Understand?"

"How do you fight a ghost?"

"I don't know. But it's not his house. It's ours. We'll just have to make him understand that, and then I think he'll go away. For now, you need to be brave, and let me know if he comes back. Okay?"

Penny stared at the house, and it stared back at her. "Okay," she whispered. "Okay, Dad. I'll try."

CHAPTER 10

Despite the summer heat, Max turned his full attention to baking. Sourdough, croissants, crepes, crullers—the kitchen was constantly filled with platters of treats and the homey smell of browning bread.

In a pleasant surprise, he also took on a commission for an old-west town set for the lobby of the county fair headquarters. It was a small but interesting job requiring research that gave him another excuse to drive to the Roseville library with Penny in tow.

Two weeks after his lunch with Emily, she agreed to meet him at the library. Penny retreated with her friends to the Young Adult section before Emily arrived. She was still not ready to see her mother in person, but had sent along another letter for Max to deliver to her. He was elbow-deep in a Roseville historic encyclopedia when Emily found him in the rows, but even before she turned the corner he knew she was there. Her perfume, the same scent she had worn since long before their marriage, had betrayed her approach.

Max had intended to chide her for arriving an hour late, but when he looked up from his book he sucked in his breath instead. The dress she wore was red, hanging on her shoulders by thin spaghetti-straps. Perfect for summer, and for teasing fusty old artists like himself.

"Hi there," he managed, squirming in his uncomfortable wooden library chair like a schoolboy.

She slid into a chair opposite his and leaned forward on her elbows. "Hi, Max. Whatcha readin'?"

"Ah, well, like I said on the phone, it's research for this new gig. The county fair committee wants a little scene de-

picting the founding of Roseville in their lobby. Someone
else is doing the people and animals, I'm just doing the
buildings. But I'm reading up on the architecture, because
I wanted to get it just right."

"Of course you did," Emily said, grinning. "You've
always been so thorough."

Max shrugged, feeling silly. His heart pounded with
excitement—but why? This was just Em, ex-wife and old
flame. Drug addict, and cheater, and…

Smoking hot.

Max's ears burned as she reached under the table and
found his thigh.

"You want to get out of here, Max?"

Max coughed. "Well, I, um…"

Emily grinned, sensing victory. "Where'd you park?"

"Dad?"

He jumped. Penny walked around the corner with
her friend Shannon, and Max slammed his book shut with
more gusto than he had intended. At the sound, a bespec-
tacled librarian poked his head around the stacks with a
disapproving scowl.

"Penny?" Emily's face had gone slack, her eyes watery
and pleading. "Oh, my baby girl! You've gotten so big!"

Penny froze. She gripped a novel with a colorful cover
to her chest, an entry in her favorite pre-teen series about
horses and boyfriends and hot summer nights.

"Um…thanks."

"I got your letters. I really appreciate them, and your
writing is so lovely. How is Copper?"

Penny looked startled, even though she had written
about Copper in her letters. It was as though she hadn't really expected the letters to reach her mother; over the last
few years, Emily had become a concept to her more than
a person. The pain ran deep. Max had to intervene. Penny

had worked hard to heal and move on since the divorce, and this encounter could undo her progress if it wasn't kept brief. Emily was unpredictable.

"Well, we have to get going. Long drive home, you know. Thanks for meeting me here, Em. Wish we'd had more time to, uh, reminisce." His ears burned again, this time with embarrassment.

Emily nodded, never taking her eyes off of Penny, watching her like a bird of prey. "Maybe next time we can all have lunch together, all three of us. Would that be okay?"

Penny shrugged.

Max moved to intercept Emily's line of sight, but turned to offer her a soft smile. "We'll at least talk about it, okay? And then I'll call. I promise."

Emily nodded gratefully. "Okay. Thanks, Max. Good luck with your, uh, little houses. I'm sure you'll do a great job."

She always knew how to coat a compliment in condescension, even under duress. It was obvious where Penny got her quick wit from.

"Thanks," he said, herding Penny and her friend back to the Young Adult section.

"Was that your mom?" Shannon asked.

"Sort of." Penny shrugged.

"She looked like you."

Penny shrugged again, looking uncomfortable.

"Hey!" Max interrupted, desperate to change the subject. "What are you up to tonight, Shannon? If you want, you girls can have a sleepover at our place."

"Really? Um…are you sure, Dad?" Penny said, surprised. He knew what she was thinking; the house might not be safe. But Max thought it was. He was complying with Puck's demands, and everything had been quiet for a while now. It was time they got on with their regular lives.

"Yep. Shannon, if you want to come over, go call your mom. I know our house is pretty far away, but I can drop you off here tomorrow afternoon. I'll need to return these library books anyway. Okay?"

The girls grinned, and Shannon ran off to find a payphone.

On the drive back to 23 Old Mine Road, Max was subjected to a solid hour of 1979 pop hits until static finally wiped out the radio station. The matching station number in Downieville played jazz, at which the girls groaned. But Max didn't let Penny change the dial after it switched over.

"It'll do you girls some good," he said. "Give you some culture!"

"Ugh, yuck."

"Yuck, indeed. But just listen to that bass line!" He turned up the volume.

"What's a bass line?"

Max let his mouth fall open in mock shock. "What's a...are you *kidding* me?"

The girls giggled, and turned their focus toward a purple diary Shannon had brought in her school pack. Max wondered what was written inside, but he was simultaneously relieved that he had no idea. Such secrets were not for the likes of him.

As he pulled the car into the driveway, he scanned the forest, the driveway, the yard. Everything looked as it had when they left; the unused fence posts were in a neat stack where he had moved them, the patio furniture was in its proper position, and the house stared meekly down at the street with its big, innocent window eyes. Of course everything was normal. What was he worried about?

Well, he had expected some retaliation, perhaps. For

bringing a stranger here. The workers installing the fence had not been welcome, but Shannon was just a girl. No threat there.

The thought that he was experimenting with the girl's life entered his mind, and he swiftly swept it away with thoughts of what he could make for dinner that the girls wouldn't turn their petite little noses up at. Hot dogs? Did kids still like hot dogs?

"What's for dinner, Dad?" Penny asked, right on cue.

"I was just thinking about that. Hot dogs?"

"Yuck."

Max sighed. Of course. "Well, I have plenty of raisin loaf and French rolls and puffed biscuits. There's also rice, and fruit."

"Fruit salad!" Penny said, hauling her bag over her shoulder.

"That sound good to you, Shannon?"

"Sure, Mr. Braun. That sounds great."

"Just call me Max, Shannon. I'll get right to work on your order, then." Max winked.

The girls ran to Penny's room after pausing to pry their shoes off by the front door.

When dinner was ready, Penny asked if she and Shannon could eat in the treehouse, so Max bagged the food to go in an old grocery tote with a bundle of napkins, forks, and a half dozen cookies wrapped in a paper towel. He sat on the back deck with a bowl of fruit salad, nibbling on sliced grapes as he eyed the hillside.

"Your dad's funny," Shannon said from inside the treehouse.

"Shh," Penny said.

Max grinned with delight. He was a funny dad who made good food. In a way, it was everything he'd always wanted.

When the forest began to darken, he took two steps up the ladder and called out to the girls.

"Time to go in, Penny."

"Aww, Dad," she whined, with her head poking out the door. "Do we have to?"

Max looked up at her, looked into her eyes. Without saying anything out loud, he reminded her why they had to go in. She nodded, and passed the grocery bag down to him.

The girls went inside first, and Max lingered, peering between the trees. He was relieved that nothing had emerged from them, of course. He told himself he wasn't surprised; if there had been any real risk, he wouldn't have let Shannon come over in the first place. Of course not.

He turned and went into the house, but in the final moment before the sliding glass door clicked shut behind him, he heard the distant cry of an elk. There was something wrong with that voice, although how he knew that was a mystery. Max was a city boy, through and through, and could hardly tell an elk from an elephant. But there was something wild about that cry, something demented. Whatever made that cry had cracked.

Max had to remind the girls to go to sleep three times, and the last time he raised his voice—but it was all an act. He didn't mind, not really. He was playing the role of caring father, but in his heart he hoped they stayed awake for hours, giggling under the blankets, chatting in the glow of the flashlights he had given them before bedtime. The late hours passed peacefully, as he had known they would. Of course they did.

In the morning, he made breakfast, which the girls ate in the treehouse. After sending up a second helping of waffles and watching the forest as they spent hours painting the treehouse ladder with loops of vines and music notes and hearts, he packed up his library books and some soda cans for the road. He also prepared a bread basket for Shannon's family; bundt cakes, mini pies in little tins (his personal favorite), and some buttery dinner rolls he was especially proud of.

As he backed the car down the drive, he caught in the corner of his eye the movement he had dreaded seeing in the trees ever since Shannon had arrived. But the disturbance was slight, and the figure which emerged was smaller than the elk or the man. It was the hare, sitting back on its haunches, staring at him with its head turned to the side. It watched as Max backed out onto Old Mine Road, put the car into drive, and sped down the hill before Penny could notice it was there.

Max sighed with relief. The social visit had been a success, even if the creature from the woods had noticed the intruder. Perhaps it didn't even mind.

"Shit!"

"Penny, watch your mouth!" Max said, as he unlocked the front door.

"But, Dad…*look!*"

"Shit!"

Water was pooled in the house entryway. A low stream had flooded the living room, coming from the direction of the hallway. Max sloshed through the water to its source; a busted pipe under the toilet. He raced to find the shutoff valve, taking big clown-steps over the water-logged carpet on his way out to the front yard.

"Check your room for anything on the floor!" he called behind as he ran for the meter.

"My notebook!" Penny cried, bolting down the hall-way.

Max cranked the shutoff lever down by the street, and strode back toward the house with one eye on the forest. The carpet was ruined, that much was clear. What about the rest of the furniture? With a pang of guilt, he hoped—just a little bit—that his new modern chair had been ruined.

"It's not too bad in here," Penny called down the hall.

"Good." Max stood with his hands on his hips and surveyed the living room. The leak must have just started a few minutes ago; the furniture was damp, but only at the legs. The kitchen was untouched. When he examined his bedroom and workshop, he found them dry. The bathroom, hallway, living room, and half of Penny's room were fairly sludgy, but most of the damage was limited to the floor.

The floor? That was forbidden territory, wasn't it?

Max's last phone call with Mr. Puck had been a month ago. It now seemed like the entire conversation had occurred in a fever dream. He knew he was being watched; the oversized hare he had seen upon leaving the house earlier that day was evidence of that. But he couldn't just leave everything as it was. The carpet would mold, and surely Mr. Puck would have a problem with that. There was only one choice; it had to be taken care of.

"All right, Penny. I want you to go out to the treehouse for a little while. Take a snack and a book with you, and anything else you might need to keep you busy for a while. I have to do some work here."

"The treehouse? Um…without you watching?"

Max nodded. "You'll be fine."

If there was going to be a problem, it was going to be right here, in the living room.

Max found a pair of leather gardening gloves in the toolbox, and some old needle-nose pliers. All the carpet would have to go, or the place would turn into a swamp. If Mr. Puck called him up on the phone, well, he would just explain the situation. What else could he do?

Max lugged the console television to the center of the room. He would have to group all the furniture together, pull up part of the carpet, then move the furniture onto the wooden boards to get to the rest. His heart pounded as he worked, either from anxiety or from the physical labor his body was unaccustomed to.

The carpet came up easily. It was heavy, but the water had loosened its tacks from the floor and they slid out of the soggy wood without any trouble. He sliced it into pieces with a box cutter, then stacked the sections outside on the driveway. As he went, he moved the furniture back into place, and pointed a fan at the wood to start drying it out.

He thought moving the sofa would be the hardest part, but it ended up being the easiest. It was lightweight, as it wasn't an expensive piece; he had picked it up for half price during an after-Christmas sale at Sears. Max preferred to sit in a chair and Penny didn't often use the living room, so the sofa saw little use. He hauled it away from the wall, tore up the damp carpet underneath, and stopped still. The pliers slipped from his numb fingers and landed with a splat on the wet floor.

Set into the wooden boards was a hatch.

The sight of it filled Max with terror. He wasn't worried about anything coming up through it, no; what frightened him was the sudden knowledge that he must go down. The answer to all the preposterous questions this house had raised over the last few weeks might lay right under that hatch, and if he ever wanted to solve the riddle of Elkstone Giveaways he had no choice but to take a chance on whatever lay behind the door.

Or, he could simply slide the sofa back into place, forget about the hatch, and keep a close eye on Penny until she eventually grew up and moved out. Couldn't be more than a few years. Perhaps that would be easier for everyone.

Max's stomach ached. Ignoring the hatch was not possible, for one simple reason; the creature had been bothering his daughter. It was talking to Penny behind his back, scaring her. If only it had left her alone, Max could have turned a blind eye, ignored what was below.

"All right," he whispered. "All right, Mr. Puck. We'll see what's behind Door Number One. Let's make a deal."

He glanced out the back door at the treehouse. Penny had turned on her flashlight, even though the sun wasn't quite down yet. She was probably reading one of the books she had checked out from the library. Good girl.

Max knelt next to the door, and slipped his glove through the metal handle. It was time for some answers.

CHAPTER 11

The room beneath the hatch smelled of mold, smoke, and ancient dust. The only illumination came through the narrow gaps in the floorboards overhead, lines of light cast by Max's own living room lamp. He squinted in the darkness, keeping his left hand firmly gripped on the ladder's middle rung.

He had expected to find a basement, but instead the room was identical in shape and size to his own living room directly above, with furniture arranged in all the same places. The style was different, outdated by about ten years. A plush olive-green sofa set faced a wood-inlaid record player built into a bench with speakers on the ends. At the far corner, where Max had put his modern chair in his own version of the room, was a little end table with an orange pot full of dead plants. Mold-streaked cushions which must have once decorated the sofa were strewn across the floor, along with shards of broken glass and dishes. Every surface—the walls, floor, and furniture—was streaked with black ash. At some time in the past, there had been a fire.

"Welcome, Max."

He bolted halfway up the ladder before he made himself stop and look back. "Who's there?" he whispered. "And what are you doing in my home?"

From a place near the entryway there was movement. A man stood there, but in the darkness all Max could see was a pallid face floating above clothing which was either black or badly burned.

"Clearly, this is not your home," the voice said. "It is mine." When he spoke, the odor of old ash wafted from his open mouth.

Max's arms ached; he needed to commit to climbing up or down. He lowered himself back to the floor, but kept both hands on the ladder.

"But why are you here, hiding out below my house? Who are you? Are you Mr. Puck?"

The man shuffled through the room, kicking aside pieces of glass and seared bits of carpet with tattered, scorched slippers. He settled into a rocking chair and folded his hands in front of its chest. "I don't know that name. But I am who you will be, if you do not leave."

"What do you mean? Leave where?"

"Leave your house. Move away. Run, if it's not already too late."

"Never. I won't do it. The house is mine. And anyway, who's going to make me?"

"Gleaner," the figure whispered.

The name chilled Max. It was like something from a dream or a movie. "Who is…" he started, but it felt dangerous to say the name out loud. "Who is that?"

"You've seen him before. In the woods. He takes many forms."

"Like an elk?"

"That's his favorite, yes. But you will always know him by the color of his eyes."

"And what does he want with me? Why does he want me to leave?"

"He doesn't. He wants you to stay. Forever."

"You still haven't told me who you are."

"I'm no one. I'm dead."

"Yeah, right."

The figure sighed. "You can't afford to be this stupid, Max. Once, long ago, I was like you. That was before."

"Before what?"

"Before the fire."

The man stood up from the rocking chair and lumbered toward Max. In the narrow strips of light filtering through the boards overhead, his face became visible in thin slices. The cheeks lay open, hollowed out by flesh-eating fire, giving a clear view of crumbling teeth set in dry, blackened gums. Patches of singed hair remained attached to his desiccated scalp, clinging to his forehead over the hollows of his eye sockets. Deep inside the holes, back where his brain should be, was a flickering blue light, glowing dull in its ruined cage of bone.

Max screamed and clapped a hand over his mouth, hoping desperately that Penny had not heard. The figure was almost close enough to touch him. Max decided it was time to make an exit while he still had enough strength to get up the ladder.

"You stay back," he babbled, hoisting himself up the rungs. "You hear? Stay away from me, and especially Penny. We're not leaving, and you can't make us!" Max heard the sputter in his voice, hating his frumpy, middle-aged weakness. "You don't scare me. And you can just pass that on to Mr. Puck, too!"

After Max slammed the hatch shut, he slid the sofa back over it and sat in his chair. He considered calling the police, but they'd never believe him. Penny was still in her treehouse, and thank god for that. She hadn't heard his little outburst at the—well, what was it, really? A walking corpse? Silly thought, that. More likely a hippie squatter, all covered in dirt. As he sat in the friendly light of his living room lamp, surrounded by furniture he'd picked out himself at the Roseville Sears Half-Price Extravaganza, his memory of the monster in the room below had already started to fade. The low level of light in the basement had confused him, no doubt. But if someone was camping out down there, they'd have to be removed, and the sooner the better. He'd have to call the cops.

When he tried to place the call, the phone was dead. A busy signal beeped over and over until the line cut off in a burst of static. He hung up and tried again, with the same result. It was a hell of a time for the phone company to have technical difficulties. Max realized for the first time just how isolated his new house in the forest felt, and how far away the neighbors were. If he shouted for help, would anyone hear?

He stood and turned to find Penny, and froze in his tracks. Standing inside the open frame of the sliding glass door was a creature which was half man, half elk. The antlers on his head were tall enough to scrape the ceiling, tracing fine lines on the plaster. Tattered animal skins lashed with leather cords around his torso and waist were pulled tight, stressed by his bulging muscles. His eyes were too large for his head, and were lit with a red glowing embers. The man's pupils were shaped like diamonds from a deck of cards.

"What do you want?" Max whispered. "Are you…are you Mr. Puck?"

The man laughed, a braying, twisted sound that rattled the windows. From his open mouth came the smell of rot.

"Of course not," the man said. "But you could say he works for me."

"What do you want?" Max demanded, forcing his voice above a whisper.

"To collect you."

"What does that…"

The elk-man laughed again, convulsing with ear-splitting peals of laughter. He turned toward the back porch, leaving a trail of hot footprints on the wood floor that steamed away the remaining water from the plumbing leak. Before descending the back steps, he turned to examine Max, amused; with his diamond eyes he judged him, a middle-aged frump, and knew he was a weak man. Max felt naked under his gaze, conscious of the extra weight around his middle and his receding hairline. Under the creature's critical eye, he felt like nothing more than easy prey.

"Bones, Max. The house has a spine," the creature hissed, "And you live on a rib. Rotten bones, deep in the earth. Where the spine ends, I live; in the bowels of the earth, in the genitals. I live and I eat the aphrodisiac, as I have since the beginning of time."

The elk-man laughed again, but his braying dissolved into dry coughs which expelled a heavy cloud of hot black smoke. Little flies, the kind Max's mother had always called no-see-ums, swarmed within the fumes. He turned and ran toward the forest, but paused halfway to the edge of the thick trees to place his hands on the ground and grow into a true elk, towering and powerful. As the animal bounded away, streaks of blood flew from its flanks to stripe the forest floor.

Max collapsed into his chair, breathing hard. Penny's flashlight still flickered in the treehouse, brighter now that the sun had set. She had not noticed the passing of the elk.

Perhaps it had never been there at all. Was he losing it?

From the direction of the hatch, Max heard a faint scuffle. A crumbling slip of paper, scorched at the edges, was being worked up through the floorboards. Max pulled the paper out and unfolded it. The words printed there made his knees go weak.

A shaky script scrawled in black ash spelled out,

"Beware the mad old god."

"Max, if you just tell me what's wrong, I'm sure I can help. But if you won't explain what's happening, I can't do a thing for you."

Max held the phone receiver in a white-knuckle grip. The line had cleared up after the elk-man was gone, but he didn't call the police. They wouldn't be able to help. He had called his ex-wife instead.

He could feel the pump of his heartbeat in the palm of his hand; if he didn't relax, he'd break the phone.

With a shuddering exhale, he closed his eyes and spoke her name with a softness he had not felt for her in years. "Emily. Thank you. But you can't help. At least, I don't think so. I shouldn't even have called you. But seriously, thank you for picking up."

"Well, if you're having some kind of mental breakdown, you were right to call me. Is Penny okay?"

"She's in her room."

"That's a start. Now, tell me exactly what happened."

As Max's heart rate slowed, he regretted making the call. He had dialed her in a panic, needing to hear a sane voice, a friendly word…but Em was the wrong choice. Before calling her, he had called Penny into the house and sent her to her room, trying to keep his voice steady. He didn't think Penny knew how scared he really was, and that was good—but he had dumped on Emily as soon as she answered the phone, an incohesive string of expletives that he could now barely recall.

"I can't tell you, I'm sorry. I know I'm the one who called you…"

Emily snorted.

"…but you can't really help. I guess I just needed to hear someone's voice."

"You're cracking, Max. You better get out of that forest before you turn into a mad old hermit up there. It can't be good for Penny, either."

"Penny's fine," Max said. "Truly, I'm sorry I called."

"Don't be like that. You can call me whenever you want, you know that. I still care for you, Max."

He went silent, listening to his own heavy breathing on the line.

"You're doing a good job with Penny," Emily continued. "She sent me a letter the other day, all on her own."

"She did?" Max was startled. That didn't sound like something Penny would do. Not right now, anyway. Not while things were so strange.

"Just got it in the mail yesterday. She sounds happy, Max."

In the background, Emily's doorbell rang.

"Sounds like you have a visitor."

"I gotta go. Call me again soon, okay? When you're more ready to talk. We'll figure this out, whatever it is."

"Sure thing, Em. Talk to you later."

Max hung up the phone, then stared at it. He had run to Emily like a boy running behind his mother's skirts. Shame burned his cheeks.

He walked through the living room toward the hall, eyeing the dark shadow under the sofa where the hatch hid. Since he had shoved the couch back against the wall, no sounds had issued from the hole. No more notes poked up through the floor. All was still.

He knocked on Penny's door. "Honey? Can we talk?"

When she peeked out, her eyes darted up and down the hallway. "Is it safe?"

"Of course it's safe. Why wouldn't it be?"

"I...uh...I don't know. You seemed a little freaked out a few minutes ago. What's up?"

"Did you write your mom a letter?"

Penny looked down at her shoes. "Yeah. I didn't tell you about it, and I'm sorry. I'm not sure why I did it. It was just something I wanted to do, kind of spur of the moment, you know? Gave the letter directly to Mr. Samson a couple days ago. Sorry."

"You have nothing to be sorry about, Penny. If you want to communicate with your mother, that's your choice. It's not even any of my business. But next time, just ask me for the stamp instead of stealing one. It's not a problem. Understand?"

Penny nodded. "Thanks, Dad."

"You're welcome, of course. But one more thing…"

Penny looked up at his face with her big, innocent eyes, and Max's resolve almost withered. But this was important.

"If she ever mentions anything about any of her bad habits…ever even hints at them…"

"I'll stop talking to her, and tell you."

"Exactly. I don't think that will happen, but her problems aren't your problems, or your fault. There's something else, too. Something that I know you don't want to talk about.

"What?"

"The elk. If that creature…that animal-thing, bothers you again…"

Penny's gaze turned steely with buried fear. "He hasn't. Not in weeks. I think he's gone."

"Perhaps, perhaps not. But if he ever talks to you again, you tell me right away. Got it?"

"Got it. What's for dinner?"

Max grinned. There was no fear in the world powerful enough to compete with the ravenous hunger of a pre-teen child. "Beef stew. Half an hour. Sound good?"

Penny nodded, and clicked her door shut.

CHAPTER 12

Emily sat at her dinner table—a cute little secondhand diner set from a café that had folded last fall—with an envelope sitting on the placemat in front of her. It was rose blush in color, not bubblegum pink, and had delicate little flowers painted on the flap. It was the stationary of a girl who was just starting to mature.

Penny's writing had improved enough to rival that of most of the professionals at the hospital where Emily worked. She was a well-spoken girl, and had made a clear effort to talk about topics she thought her estranged mother might be interested in; the wildlife in the forest near the new house, the hot weather, and what President Carter had said on television about the oil crisis. She wanted to know if Emily liked Barbara Streisand, and whether she had seen *The Black Stallion* at the movie theater yet. So many unspoken words lay hidden under the ones she wrote: Do you still love Dad? Do you miss me? Do you still love me?

Emily traced the return address with a manicured fingernail. 23 Old Mine Road. It was printed in tacky gold leaf on a lick-back stamp label, the cheap kind you get by sending in a mail-order form clipped from a magazine. Max probably had them printed up for his little model business. Had Penny stolen it from her father's desk, along with the stamp? She was a good girl, but she was as private as her father, and Emily thought it was likely she hadn't told him about the letter.

The address didn't show up on any maps, but she didn't think Penny had written it wrong. Penny was too smart for that kind of mistake. So what was going on, over at that house in the woods? Emily knew Max had no business owning his own house. She didn't begrudge him his good fortune, no matter how it had happened; she really did hope for the best for him, silly as the man was. And for Penny, of course. A growing girl needed a secure home with a yard, not a crummy bachelor's pad.

She took a sip of wine, and glanced around at her own stark apartment. It was plain, almost empty except for a few necessities. The microwave in the kitchen saw more use than the oven, and the couch more than the bed. Two buckets of chartreuse wall paint sat atop a pile of clean tarps in the corner, next to paintbrushes which still had the tags on them. Just one project in an endless line of them that she had started and never completed. If sober living was so healthy, why could she never find the mental or physical energy to finish anything? The sterile white walls remained empty, decorated only with generic pictures of better places; a sunset, a mountain, a waterfall. They had come with the frames.

So many memories in this place, most of them bad. Ex-boyfriends, bad drugs, good drugs. Risky business. Not a place to raise a young girl. Max had been right all along about that. Emily was no good for Penny.

But maybe Emily could be good for Max.

She still remembered Clive's number, didn't even have to check the Rolodex. That old cowboy always did have a soft spot for her, and not just because of a few hot nights in the summer of 1973 in the back of his truck parked behind the Stop-N-Shop. There was something between them that clicked just right, despite the difference in their ages. If he had been a few years younger, like a decade or so, she might have ended up moving in with him. Maybe even squeezed out a kid or two. He was that sweet.

"'Ello," he answered the phone, speaking in that gravelly voice Emily had found so appealing in the weeks after leaving her soft husband.

"Clive, it's Emily. How you doing?"

"Emmy! It's great to hear from you, sweetie. I'm about as good as I've ever been. What trouble have you been getting into lately?"

"None. Or, almost none. Believe it or not." Emily grinned.

"I don't."

"Well I suppose that's understandable. But I have a favor to ask."

"Now *that* I believe. If you're looking for a hookup, I…"

"No, I'm clean. Have been for a while."

"Good for you." Clive's voice was warm, approving.

"I need to borrow a car. That old truck you have, if it still works. Got an errand to run."

Clive sighed into the phone. "And this hasn't got anything to do with any of your vices? You sure, sweetie? This dog's too old to get mixed up in anything new."

"Promise. Cross my heart, hope to die."

"Well, all right then. I'll swing by tomorrow and pick you up around two o'clock. Then you drop me off home and take the truck, and do whatever you need to do. But don't keep it more than a few days. I need it for next week's hay haul. Good enough?"

"Good enough. Thank you so, *so* much, Clive. I'll see you tomorrow."

"Yup."

On her drive to Downieville, she almost hit a deer. Max's new house was really out there; the trees came right up to the road, thick and ordered as a marching band. The deer bounded out from between the trees and stopped in the middle of the highway to whip its head around and stare at her. For a moment its eyes reflected her headlights with an eerie red glow. She swerved and missed the animal's body, but clipped its slender antler with the left side mirror, sending it spinning onto the pavement with a sickening crack.

She knew she should stop and drag the animal to the side of the road before it was hit by another car, but her squeamishness got the better of her. It would be a gory mess, for sure. Maybe not even dead yet, but kicking and crying...

No. No way. Not today.

As she accelerated away from the scene, she went to turn off the headlights and discovered they were already off. The red in the deer's eyes must have been reflecting something else, like the sunset or another car's lights. Weird.

While 23 Old Mine Road had not appeared on any maps she could find, 21 Old Mine Road was at the nearby intersection with Pine Avenue and she felt she could safely assume 23 was its neighbor. On her way up the hill she passed a surly mailman walking on foot, carrying bulging bags of mail. She waved as she passed, but he only scowled back. The old coot probably knew the full name and backstory of every person on the mountain, and had recognized her as a stranger. Oh, well.

21 Old Mine Road was a light blue house with a brick chimney and a messy jacaranda tree that covered the lawn and half the street with sticky purple flowers every time a breeze shook its branches. The north side of 21's property ran up the hill a ways before ending in a neatly manicured border where its well-maintained grass lawn met with a more rugged lot; must be Max's property. He never was big on maintenance, even when he lived in an apartment.

It came as no surprise he didn't bother to take care of the sprawling lawn on his new lot.

As she had suspected, 23 Old Mine Road was on the other side of that ill-kept acreage. She found the house number tacked onto the front wall near the stoop of an odd flat-roofed house that somehow managed to seem both rustic and modern, old yet new. Massive windows overlooked a sloping circular driveway that arced down to the street at both ends, and at the apex of the curve was a pile of soggy-looking squares of molding carpet. A mangled fence weaved into the forest on the right side of the house, marked by electric-blue ties as if the broken fence was not sufficient evidence of the property line. Parked before the carpet pile was Max's old 1968 Ford station wagon, a hideous green thing she had not been able to talk him out of buying during their marriage. Her choice had been the Mustang, but Max said at the time that he was hoping for more kids, and there wouldn't be enough room for them in the back. If they'd known then what they knew now, she could have had the Mustang.

Emily parked Clive's truck behind the station wagon and checked her lipstick in the mirror. She was here for Max, not Penny, she reminded herself. But just in case the girl wanted to see her, she ought to look tidy, if not matronly. Emily hoped Penny would be as chatty in person as she had been in her letter, but she promised herself she wouldn't push too hard. Let the girl come to her, in her own way and time.

From the forest stepped a deer. It was much larger than the one she had clipped on the highway, but it had that same red glow in its eyes. Its sides heaved in and out with heavy breathing, and it flared its nostrils. A trickle of blood traced the skin at the split of its nose, ran down its lip, and dripped to the ground.

When the front door of the house opened, the deer turned and bounded into the woods.

"Mom?" It was Penny, standing hesitant on the stoop.

"Baby-girl!" Emily exited the car but did not move any closer. She wanted Penny to take the first step.

She was not disappointed. Seconds later, Penny was squeezing her tight, wetting her blouse with tears. "I'm... so glad...to see you," she gasped. "But what are you doing here? Did Dad ask you to come?"

"No. Just a mother's intuition, I guess," Emily said. "I enjoyed your letter, but got a feeling from it that you might want a visit, so here I am. I hope that's okay."

"Em?"

Max stood in the open doorway with his hands on his hips. He frowned, then noticed Penny's tight embrace and shrugged. "Welcome to our home, I guess."

"Can she stay overnight?" Penny asked her father, sniffling. "She drove so long to get here."

Max spread his hands open and shook his head. "I... Penny..."

"Nothing...nothing bad will happen. It'll be okay," Penny said. These statements were directed at her father with a cryptic look that made it plain to Emily that it might not, in fact, be okay. What was going on here?

"If the answer is no, Max, I understand," Emily said. "Really, it's no pressure. I just wanted to see both of you, that's all."

"No, no, you can stay. It'll be fine. Do you have any, uh, luggage?"

"Only one bag. Don't worry about that, though. I'll grab it later. First I want to see this beautifully painted treehouse I've heard all about!"

Penny grabbed Emily's hand, and a jolt of joy struck her. Her daughter's hand in her own was something she thought she would never experience again.

Max watched Penny and Emily from behind the sliding glass door with his arms crossed.

How had she found the house? Max had spent hours at the post office, arguing with them about his lack of mail and his apparently unlisted address. It seemed that every letter sent to the house was somehow lost, which was too wild a coincidence to happen every single day. Checks which had been mailed to him by clients had simply disappeared from the system. If his most recent job had not been for a customer in nearby Oakland, he might have had to drive all the way to another state to collect payment.

Leave it to Emily to crack the code. However she had found the address, she was here now. And the truth was that Max was glad; there was a lonely feeling to the house, inherent in its position on the hillside and apparent non-existence in the city records. After years of apartment living, the solitude of a separated home was new to him.

Max watched Emily ascend the treehouse ladder to peek inside at the murals painted by Penny's careful hand. When Penny had run out of room for pictures, she had started to add garlands of dried flowers, strings of beads, and crochet ribbons. It had a certain hippie vibe Max thought Emily would probably appreciate.

She seemed sober enough, too. Max knew what she looked like when she was high, and this wasn't it. Her smile was genuine, and her eyes were present in the moment. He felt proud of her for a moment, before chiding himself; his ex had showed up unannounced, and he was just happy that she wasn't hopped up on coke. How much lower could his expectations possibly be for this woman?

He slid the door open and called out, "Dinner in five!"

"What we havin'?" Penny called back.

"Tacos!"

"Yay!"

When they had all taken their seats at the table, an awkward silence fell. They had not sat together like that, as a family gathered for dinner, since the last night of Max and Emily's marriage—and that had not been a good night. Emily had been sniffling, as she often did in those days, wiping at her nose and her watery eyes. Penny was too young to understand what was wrong with her mommy, but old enough to know not to ask.

"Dig in," Max said, picking up a taco. He bit into it with a loud crunch that made Penny giggle.

"Thanks, Max. I know I just kind of...showed up. That was probably rude, I know. But I..."

"It's fine, Emily. I'm glad you can see for yourself that Penny is living in a real home, just like I said."

Emily blushed. "That's not why I'm here. I believed you, really."

"It's fine."

"Anyone want a glass of wine?" Penny asked, rising from her chair. "I'm going to get a soda."

"No thank you," Emily said. "I rarely drink, these days."

"I'll have a bourbon," Max said. "Thanks, kiddo."

After dinner, Max and Emily sat in chairs on the back patio, smoking. Max had always admired the causal way Emily held her cigarette; sort of loose, letting it droop like she didn't care if she dropped the thing. It got his attention, every time. She was a sexy smoker.

"Why are you really here, Em?"

"I'm not actually here for Penny. I know that's what you were thinking. But I promise I'm not being pushy. I'll leave it up to her."

"Okay. Why, then?"

"I'm here to see you."

"Yeah? What do you need from me this time?"

Emily blushed, then frowned. "That's not fair."

"Isn't it?"

It was fair, and they both knew it. How many favors had Max done for her, over the years? And how few had she ever repaid?

"Yes, it's fair. But I really am here to see you. I just…" Emily put out her cigarette. "Do you miss me at all, Max?"

Max frowned. "I miss having company. I miss having a partner. But whether I actually miss *you*, in particular, well…"

"Well?"

"I'm not sure about that." Max mashed his cigarette in the ashtray, popping out its cherry. It sat winking in the twilight, glowing red like the elk's eyes.

"Well, what about this?" Emily moved from her chair to kneel on the porch in front of Max. She ran her hands up his inner thighs, leaning forward to ensure he had a good view down her blouse. "Do you miss this?"

"I might…maybe. Miss that," he whispered.

"Yeah?"

"Maybe."

She rubbed his legs, moving her hands nearer to his zipper, massaging him in a way he had not felt since before she had left him. But before she moved her hands to grip the bulge below his pants button, she grabbed his hands and stood, pulling him to his feet.

"Where we goin'?" he asked, his voice husky and low.

"Somewhere more private."

Emily pulled him down the steps, towards the forest. He mumbled a warning or protestation, but he was too eager to follow for his words to make sense. She tugged him toward the treehouse ladder and stood on the bottom rung, grinning back at him, watching him watching her. But before she could take another step up, his eyes cleared.

"No. Not up there."

"Why not? You're a carpenter, kind of. I'm sure you built it sturdy enough."

"It's not that. Penny's treehouse is…it's sacred."

Emily nodded. She took his hand again and pulled him deeper into the pines, following the mangled, nonsensical remains of the fence. In a tiny clearing where the needles were sparse, she pulled him close and kissed him. When her lips touched his he surrendered to her, giving up his reservations about her and about the forest. His hands slipped under her blouse, seeking a bra strap, and found none. He groaned his excitement into her mouth, then pulled her blouse off over her head.

Emily let him lay her down in the dirt. The decadence of it, out in the open and within view of their daughter's treehouse, made his heart pound in his chest. Max knew he was older and softer than most of her suitors, but tonight that didn't matter. Tonight they were both young again.

As Max rediscovered her body, kissing and rubbing and moaning with joyful relief, an elk stepped out of the woods. It moved close without fear, without making a sound, puffing two jets of fog from its nostrils. Its eyes glowed red as it watched Emily pull off his pants, strip off his shirt.

The pupils at the center of the elk's eyes were shaped like diamonds.

Max wanted to stop her, but he found himself unable to speak; his astonishment at their strange spectator was overlapped by his intense desire, and the combination of conflicting emotions rendered him mute. She rolled him onto his back and straddled him, redirecting his wandering attention as she lowered herself onto his body. When he entered her she orgasmed almost instantly, screaming in the woods like a wild thing. And as she exploded, the elk looked on with eerie calm, dripping a stream of spit and blood from its mouth. It did not turn back towards the thick trees until Max also cried out with pleasure, seconds later, with more passion than he ever had during his short, bitter marriage.

CHAPTER 13

It was a two-bourbon day.

Not great, but not really very bad, either. Max's bizarre night with Emily had left him confused, worried, and persistently horny all morning. Penny sensed something was wrong at breakfast and had asked where her mother had gone, probably suspecting they'd had a fight. But he had explained that Emily had needed to leave early, even though she had wanted to stay. And that was the truth.

Max was distracted enough by his warm memories from the previous night that he didn't notice the way Penny was tugging at her shirt sleeve, picking at her food, chewing her nails. He wondered if Emily would ever pay him back the money he lent her. And other than money, what did she want? She was sober, that was obvious. And she hadn't asked him for any specific favors—in fact, it could be argued that she had given him one. Although she had seemed plenty into it herself. Perhaps she...

"Dad."

"Hmm."

"Dad!"

Max jumped. "What? You don't have to raise your voice. I'm right here."

"No, you're not. You're not really here, and I need you to be."

Max frowned at Penny, and noticed the frayed hem at her wrist and her uneaten breakfast. "What's wrong?"

Penny stared down at her oatmeal. "You said to tell you if he came back. Well, he did. Last night."

Max dropped his spoon. "When? When, exactly, did he come back?"

"I don't know exactly what time. It was after dinner, while you and Mom were smoking out back. Or maybe just a little while after that."

Oh, god. The creature had come to the house while he and Emily were out in the woods. "What did he say to you?"

"I can't remember most of it. But he was in the shape of a big rabbit again. I know it was definitely him because of, you know, the eyes. The only other thing I remember was that he said I could stay, but you couldn't. He told me I would go below, and you would go away. What does that mean?"

"Below..." Max whispered. His eyes darted toward the sofa in the living room.

"Do you know what he was talking about?"

Max stood. "No idea. But go to your room for now, Penny. I'll clean up the table, just go."

"Am I in trouble?" Penny whispered. Tears formed in her eyes.

"No! Oh, honey, not at all." Max hugged her, and kissed her forehead. "Just take Copper and don't come out of your room until I say you can. Okay?"

"Okay. Um, Dad?"

"Yes?"

"I love you."

"I love you too, honey. Always and forever."

His old tool belt was in the station wagon's trunk, next to a rusted flashlight. The light worked, but it took him half an hour to scavenge enough batteries to fill the casing in the handle. He considered bringing his hammer along as a weapon, maybe hooked to the belt, but dismissed the idea; whoever was below the floor was already dead. Further physical violence was unlikely to be a threat to any creature such as that.

After ensuring Penny and Copper were locked behind her bedroom door, he slid the sofa out from the wall. The hatch appeared untouched since he had closed it last. The person below had not tried to escape, and no more notes had been jammed up through the floorboards.

With a final glance toward the hall, Max opened the hatch and clicked on the flashlight. Aiming it into the lower room, he called out softly, "I'm coming down now. Don't try anything funny."

When he received no answer, he descended, gripping the flashlight in his teeth.

He could see more of the room this time, with the aid of the extra light. It was strikingly similar to his own living room, not just in shape and size but in the details, too. Positioned on either side of the front door were two huge glass windows like his own, but these looked out only into the earth. Dirt and roots pressed up against the glass, like an ant farm wall. As he had suspected, everything in the room had been scorched. A fire had once torn through this place, and quickly. Only crumbling black remnants of the curtains remained. The floor was the least damaged, a sturdy construction of wooden boards, the same as his own.

"Welcome back," the burned man in the rocking chair said.

"I need to know who you really are. And why you're talking to my girl. If you're a ghost—and I don't believe in ghosts, mind you—then I need you to get the hell out of my house. I banish thee, or whatever. You hear?"

The man chuckled. "I'm not a ghost. And I'm not the one talking to Penny."

"How do you know her name?" Max demanded.

"I live right underneath you. I hear all sorts of things."

The man bowed his head, and Max had an idea that if his eyes had not been burned out of his skull long ago, there would be a knowing glint in them.

"Not anymore. You're leaving tonight. Now."

"I'm not. Believe me, I would leave if I could. But he won't let me."

"Who? Mr. Puck?"

The burned man laughed. "You're really fixated on this Mr. Puck fellow, aren't you? No, the one who would stop me is the mad old god. Surely you've met him by now."

"You're talking about Gleaner."

The burned man flinched. "Say that name quietly, Max, or else not at all."

"Tell me what is going on. Tell me right now. Why is this place burned?"

"I did it myself. It was a mistake. I thought I could get out that way, but I was wrong."

"And so you're dead now? Died in the fire, I assume, but you're talking to me anyway. And despite all of that, you say you aren't a ghost."

"I don't know the answer to that. But they might." The burned man tapped his foot on the floorboards. "They've been here longer than I."

"Who?"

"The ones downstairs." The burned man gestured toward the corner of the room, where a hatch was set into the floorboards.

"You mean there's another level below? Another room like this one?"

"The downstairs neighbors. Everyone's got them, although I haven't visited in years. They've gone mad with grief, and I find them very unpleasant to talk to."

"Mad..." Max mumbled with numb lips. The way the

burned man spoke made him feel like he was missing the
meaning of everything he said. Each sentence made sense
on its own but the sentiment behind them was thick with
riddles, the answers to which were reliant on knowledge
Max could not begin to guess at.

"Perhaps," the burned man said, "They are the ones
who speak to Penny. But it's not me, I assure you. I'm a
private man."

Max walked to the hatch. It was near the hallway,
which, like the living room, mirrored his own. What was
in those rooms at the end of that hall? Did the burned
man have a burned bedroom?

"Fine. I'll ask them myself."

"Good luck," the burned man said. "They are not as
eloquent as I."

The hatch had a knob, instead of a handle like the one
in his own living room. Max turned it and pulled, but it
did not budge until he worked its rusty hinges loose. The
wood squealed as it separated from its frame, an alarming
noise in the quiet room. Below the opening a ladder was
fastened to a wall with oxidized metal brackets. It was
thinner and older than the one below his own hatch, and
covered in slick wet moss.

With his flashlight in his mouth, Max descended. The
ladder creaked under his weight, but held. A splinter drove
itself into the webbing between his thumb and palm, but
until he reached the floor he could do nothing about it.

By the time his feet touched the boards, all thoughts
of the splinter had left his mind. The room was rotten. Its
shape was identical to the two levels above, but the walls
were rippling with mush, sagging under the weight of
a forest of algae. Mushrooms clustered in every corner,
popped out from the furniture stitching, filled the gaps
between the cushions in the couch. Max breathed hard

in humid air with sparse oxygen and a thick reek of black mold. In the center of the room, between a set of orange cushion chairs and an ugly vinyl sofa, was a coffee table shaped like a flying saucer; classic 1950s decor. A dead cockroach the size of a mouse rested upside-down atop a souvenir coaster.

"Howdy, mister," a voice said. It was wet and guttural, with a clogged sound that made Max want to clear his own throat.

"Hi," he whispered. "I'm Max, from…upstairs."

"How lovely," a different voice said. This one was feminine and raspy, like snapping-dry rose vines. "A visitor."

"We overheard your chat with Desmond," the lower voice said. "About your poor daughter Penny."

"It wasn't us," the feminine voice said. "Those days are behind us now."

"What do you mean?" Max said, coughing. He could feel spores rush down his throat with every breath. Pressure built in his chest as congestion set in, squeezing his lungs.

"Desmond, the poor burned fella upstairs," the guttural voice said. "You know."

"I…know him," Max said. "Yes. Are you Mr. Puck?"

A figure emerged from the darkness of the hallway. It shuffled forward on legs which were bloated, testing the seams of its tattered denim trousers. In the places where the fabric was torn, white skin bulged through, coated in slime and specks of mud like a mushroom cap poking up from a forest floor. A long beard hung down over an amusingly outdated western plaid, complete with mother-of-pearl buttons and a bolo tie. Black mold bloomed in every hem, every crevice. The man's face hovered above the collar, a sallow full moon topped with a cowboy hat. Puss-smeared eyes floated in overlarge sockets among strips of moss sprouting out from under the eyelids.

Max took a step back on the marshy carpet, and ran into the ladder. The feel of it at his back filled him with courage, reminding him that he could leave here whenever he wanted to. This was a chance to get some answers, and he shouldn't waste it.

Before Max could open his mouth, the man spoke.

"Ten years," he said.

"What?"

"Every ten years. And if my math is correct, you only have a few weeks left."

"I have no idea what you're talking about."

"The stack will collapse, taking you with it. See?"

Max shook his head. "The stack?"

"Dear, leave poor Max alone," the feminine voice drifted from the hallway. "You'll anger him," she whispered. "I don't want to anger him again."

"Him? You don't mean me, do you? You're talking about the elk. You don't want to make Gleaner mad, is that it?"

The feminine voice gasped, and something dropped to the floor.

"Don't say his name so loud, boy," the man said. "Not if you value your life."

"Tell me what you know about him," Max said. "Speak quickly and plainly. I'm tired of playing games, and I'm not afraid of ghosts, if that's what you are."

The man looked surprised. His eyes opened wider, and a tiny white worm poked its head out from his tear duct. "Ghosts! Ha! If it were only that simple."

"Talk to me! Now!"

"I don't think we're ghosts," the feminine voice said. She leaned her face into the light. It was covered in a network of fine roots. "But perhaps Mickey is a ghost. He's different. He passed before the stack fell. Would you like to meet Mickey?"

"No. I just want to know who has been talking to my daughter. And we won't leave our house, if that's what you're doing. You can't scare us away. It won't work."

"We'd never do that!" the woman laughed, walking toward the kitchen. "Come on over and make a new friend." Her clammy, bloated hand beckoned him with cranberry-red nails.

Max did not follow her, but he sidestepped until he had a view of the kitchen from the living room. It was, as he expected, similar to his own, but even more inundated by fungus and mushrooms than the living room was. A swarm of gnats whirled over a counter loaded with flat mats of creeping tendrils. The sink was piled with puffy morels, the ceiling festooned with hairlike roots connected by thick spiderwebs. On a silver filament, a chunky spider lowered itself to land on Max's shoulder. When he tried to brush it off, it grasped his finger in its legs and would not let go until he popped its body on the soggy drywall.

"Mickey," the woman called in a sweet, singsong voice. "Wake up and meet the new neighbor, my baby boy." She stopped in front of the refrigerator with her hand resting her hand on the latch. "Ah, my son, my Mickey. How long has it been?"

When she opened the door, Max gagged. The refrigerator was packed full of Mickey. His legs were cut off and jammed in alongside his torso like cigars in a box. His arms, severed at the elbows, were tucked by his cheeks on each side of his head. So much moss had grown on his body it was difficult to tell what he had been wearing or what he had looked like; it connected him to the inner walls of the refrigerator, creating a single mass of organisms grown from a combination of living and dead matter.

Unlike his caregivers, Mickey was beyond speech; his mouth was a mess of spidery lichen crusts, grown large enough to force his jaw open in a perpetual scream.

"Gleaner did this," the woman said, turning to look at Max with desperate grief in her eyes. "Gleaner did it, all because our poor Mickey tried to leave the stack."

"Shush now, dear," the man said. "He'll hear you."

Max dropped his flashlight, but even from its position on the floor it was bright enough to guide him to the ladder. He bolted up, ignoring the creaking of the sodden wooden rungs, and slammed open the hatch into the burned man's room. He did not stop there; sprinting for the next hatch, he waved off Desmond's feeble greeting and burst up into his own living room, throwing the hatch open hard enough to dent the wall.

Penny stood at the entry to the hallway, gripping her notebook to her chest.

"Dad? What's wrong?" Her eyes were open wide, staring at the grime and ash and mold which caked his clothes.

"Nothing," Max said. "It's just an old basement," he huffed, trying to catch his breath. He shoved the sofa back over the hatch until it slammed into the wall.

"Stop lying to me."

Max looked up at his daughter, startled. "Lying? Honey, I…"

"You lied about the workers who installed the fence, and you're lying about what's under that hatch. I already know you did. So just stop it!"

Max sighed. "I'm sorry."

"Don't be sorry. Just fix it. I say we leave here, right now. Something is wrong with this house, and you know it. It's not safe. Can we please just go?"

Max looked at his young daughter's brave face. Her

arms were still crossed over her chest, pressing her note-book to her body; the very image of resolution. She was not yet an adult, but her childhood was passing quickly… and she was right.

"Pack a bag. We'll leave as soon as you're ready."

But where would they go?

CHAPTER 14

Penny sat in the back of the station wagon, holding Copper. Max tossed two suitcases into the trunk before pausing in the front yard for a moment, looking up at the house. Despite everything, he would miss it. But it really had been too good to be true.

"Dad! Come *on*. Please, let's just go."

Max nodded, digging his keys out of his pocket. He sat in the driver's seat, and turned over the ignition. The Ford rumbled and started just as it always had, despite sitting for a week. It had always been such a reliable old machine.

But it only ran for five or six seconds before something snapped under the hood. Penny screamed, and Copper scraped his claws down her forearm in a panic, leaving a row of angry red scratches. By the time Max and Penny tumbled out, smoke was billowing from the car.

"No, no…" Penny sobbed. "Why did he do that?"

"Must be some kind of mechanical malfunction. Damn!"

"No, it was him. The wapiti did it, because he doesn't want us to leave."

Max shook his head. "Maybe. I just don't know, Penny. I'm not sure we should jump to that conclusion. Let's go back inside for now, and…"

Penny sniffed. "No. Let's go anyway, Dad. Right *now*." She started walking across the yard toward the property line, with Copper pulling on his leash in front.

Max was struck with panic, and felt his breath leave him. Something was wrong with what she was doing. It wasn't allowed. Penny would be punished if she did not turn around, although he didn't know how he knew.

"Penny! No! You have to stop before you…"

She reached the point where the grass changed color from pale yellow-green to lush emerald, and stepped over into the neighbor's yard. A moment later, the elk burst from the edge of the forest at a full charge with its head down. Snot and blood flew in streamers from its nostrils as it aimed for Penny, flashing its red diamond eyes. Penny screamed and jumped back from the property line before the elk could impale her with its antlers, but a massive hoof landed on Copper's back, snapping his spine. The cat died, twitching in its tiny harness.

"Penny!" Max roared, charging toward her. The elk was turning around to begin another pass when Max reached her and picked her up, hoisting her over his shoulder to carry her back to the house. He ignored her kicking and protests; she wanted to go back and get Copper, to make sure he was okay.

The elk shifted its direction to match Max's sprint across the lawn, and lowered its head to charge again at full speed. Max, running faster than he ever had before in his life, put the smoking station wagon between himself and the animal. He fumbled with his keys at the front door lock as Penny screamed on the step beside him. The elk bellowed in mad excitement, and even amid the chaos Max remembered his night with Emily in the woods. Over Emily's passionate vocalizations, there had been another sound. It was one which, at the time, he had tried to ignore. He understood now that the elk had always been watching them, just as it must have been watching today as they prepared to leave. It was always present.

He jammed the key in the lock, pulled Penny inside, and slammed the door shut just as the elk rounded the station wagon. Max thought it would veer away toward the forest, but instead it stood breathing hard outside the door, staring at the house, waiting to see if they would reemerge.

"Go away!" Max yelled at it through one of the big front windows. "Get out of here!"

In response, the elk reared back, kicking its front hooves into the air in front of its chest. Its neck shortened, as did its legs, and its torso narrowed until it was a man wrapped in skins with antlers protruding from his head. He stood at the door in a cloud of black smoke, heaving and grinning, enjoying the rush of the hunt. His dark silhouette outside the window showed a nonsensical blend of animal and man.

"Maxwell Braun!" the elk-man shouted. "You are bound to this house. You are bound to me!"

Max held Penny close, shaking his head. "Let Penny go! Whatever you want from me, I don't care. I'll stay, if that's what you need. But please, let her leave!"

The elk-man laughed in a high, shrieking voice that did not match his bulky stature. It sounded like insanity.

"The girl is bound to me as well. But I have a gift for her."

"I don't want it!" Penny screamed. "Go away!"

Something heavy struck the front door.

"Yes. I will go, but you will stay," the elk-man said. "That is how it has always been."

The elk-man left then, and his shadow disappeared from the front-facing windows. The smoke from the car thinned as the flames died down. Max opened the front door, and found what had struck it; the elk-man's gift to Penny. It was Copper, mangled and bloody, with his harness leash twisted around his body over and over like a mummy's wraps.

"What is it, Dad?" Penny asked, rubbing her eyes.

"Nothing. It's nothing, Penny, just…"

"You're lying to me again."

"No." Max said. He opened the door wide to show her what she wanted to see.

"Oh no, oh no…" Penny wailed.

The cat twitched. It rolled over, whipping its tail for balance, and extended its two front arms straight out to pull itself forward with its tiny claws. The sight of it moving filled Max with dread; the cat was dead. He had no doubt of this. It was bent almost in half, crushed where the elk's hoof had landed on its little spine. Its back legs were bound up in the leash, but the front ones moved as it pulled itself across the door's threshold.

Penny fainted. Max caught her before her head hit the floor, but took the opportunity to scoop up Copper and tuck him into a cardboard box left over from the move. When she woke up, the cat would be gone…and Max would have to lie to her again. And he'd have to do a better job, this time.

Max left Penny sleeping in her bed and sat in his modern chair, holding the first bourbon of the day in his trembling hand. They were trapped in their house—no, it wasn't really their house though, was it? It was the elk-man's house, always had been. It belonged to Gleaner.

Penny slept for hours. Max was anxious for her to wake, but he decided to leave her alone; the girl was exhausted. Also, he dreaded the conversation they would have when she regained consciousness. Would he tell her the truth, or would he lie to her again? Which was worse? It seemed like something a good father should know by instinct, but he had no idea.

Copper was dead, yet not dead. Max had buried the squirming cat near the workmen's grave, hoping the internment would give the creature its rest. Penny didn't need to know exactly what had happened to the men, either, but perhaps he needed to tell her. It was selfish of him, perhaps, but he didn't want to be alone in his fear anymore.

"Dad?" Penny walked into the living room, rubbing her eyes. Her voice was thick and groggy. "Where's Copper?"

Max had hoped he would have more time to think, but the abrupt question startled the truth out of him, bringing his indecision to an abrupt end. "He's dead, honey. The elk got him. Remember?"

Penny's face turned stony. Her arms dropped to her sides, limp, as her memory rushed back. Max would have preferred that she cry, but instead she became serious, almost stoic. "I remember. He...I mean the elk...he's not going to let us ever leave again, is he?"

"No. I don't think so."

"What are we going to do?"

Max shook his head. "I don't know."

A soft rustling sound came from under the sofa. Penny screamed, and backed up until she ran into the living room wall. "What's that? Is he back already?"

Max sighed. "No. It's just Desmond." He pulled the sofa away from the wall and picked up the scrap of paper which had been slipped between the boards.

In spidery cursive, the note read: "*The only way out is down.*"

CHAPTER 15

Betsy's sister said she didn't have the guts to work in debt collection. Betsy was determined to prove the bitch wrong.

Most of the customers weren't so bad, anyway. Some cried a little bit, and most made promises they and Betsy both knew wouldn't be kept. More than anything, it was a job of paperwork to file and forms to fill out, red tape and bureaucracy—and that kind of work suited Betsy right down to her toes.

Wednesday was her first day wearing her new dress, a dark blue wrap-around with big black polka-dots. She had blown her bonus on a shopping spree at JCPenney, but the results had been worth it. Mr. Potter had complimented her that very morning, in fact, which was something he had never done before. He was single and wealthy, and handsome to boot. In the past he had made it clear that he favored slim women, but perhaps she had a chance with him if she dressed up nice enough. His open admiration of her figure that very morning proved she should keep trying. Things were really looking up.

Today's route would likely be a challenging one; the first client on her list was labeled as a missing person with a dead account. Normally the agency would not pursue such an out-of-date debt, but the amount was outstanding, way up in the thousands. The old address wasn't even on the map anymore, but Betsy thought she could find it. She was quite a clever detective when it came to tracking down clients. Her bitch of a sister had been wrong about that, too.

21 Old Mine Road was a nice blue house at the intersection with Pine, and 23 was just a little bit up the

hill from there. Easy-peasy. Betsy pulled her sedan into a circular driveway with an odd assortment of junk at the top; a burnt-up station wagon with scorch marks around the hood, a pile of moldy carpet, and splotches of red paint that looked a little like blood—but of course it couldn't be. Anyway, most of her clients lived in somewhat down-trodden dwellings. She usually encountered some level of squalor.

After parking behind the busted car, she dug through her files. The collection was for a man called Desmond Rudder, who owed $3092.86 on an overextended credit account. Betsy "*tsked*" to herself. Some people just shouldn't be granted credit cards.

With the file tucked under her arm she approached the front door, tip-toeing through the red paint which was not quite dry yet. It had a metallic odor to it, but perhaps that was a lingering smell from the station wagon which still issued tendrils of smoke. The car fire had been recent.

The property was an especially bad one. The front lawn had not been maintained at all. Most of the grass was dead or dying, and part of it looked like it had been trampled by a bull. The red paint continued up the stoop, and after she ascended the front steps she stopped short. A large splash of paint was centered on the door, and it had clumps of fine hair stuck in it. It was truly disgusting how some people lived.

Grimacing, she pressed the doorbell, trying not to snap her fingernail on the tiny button. A chime rang inside the house, the cheap electronic kind that didn't quite sound like real bells. The door cracked open, and a frightened eye peeked through the gap. But Betsy was used to clients who greeted her with fear; it was all part of the job.

"I am looking for a Mr. Desmond Rudder. He has an outstanding account of..."

"You have to go, right *now*. Run!"

"Pardon me?"

"You're not safe. Please, ma'am, just get back in your car before it's too late."

"Are you threatening me, sir? I've cracked tougher nuts than you, believe-you-me. I'm here to collect payment on behalf of CaliNet Savings and Loan. Are you Mr. Desmond Rudder?"

"No. I'm not. He's…uh, he moved away."

"Well, if you will just provide me with his forwarding address I will leave you alone."

"Wait a second, I'll be right back."

Betsy huffed. The least the man could do was invite her inside. The rudeness of these people out in the forest neighborhoods was the hardest part of her job, really. They all thought they were special, sitting up on their hilltops, hiding out in the trees. But really they were more like cave people than anything else. By the time the man returned, Betsy was almost considering taking off her heels—but she didn't want to get paint on her stockings.

"Here," the man whispered, poking a slip of paper through the crack. "Don't read it yet. Just get in your car and drive as fast as you can. Read it when you're far away from here."

Betsy sniffed at the man and unfolded the paper. "What…"

There was no address on the paper, just a note. Something was scrawled there about police, and help. She couldn't make it all out.

"This isn't what I asked for, whoever-you-are. I simply won't leave without either a check for the amount due, or a forwarding address. Got it?"

"Just go!" the man wailed. "You have to go now, before he comes back!"

Somewhere deep in the forest, a tree shook with a violent seizure. The man's eyes darted toward a mangled fence at the side of the yard. "It's too late. You're out of time. Run! Now!" He closed the door, and a lock clicked.

"Hmph! I'll be back, you hear me, Mr. Rudder? You're only making this harder on yourself. I don't play games!"

Betsy spun on her toe and picked her way back through the gooey paint splotches toward her car. The nerve of some people…

A large deer stepped from the forest. Its attention was fixated on her; under a wide spread of antlers were two burning eyes that followed her movement down the driveway. It was too far away to be a threat, but the sight of it filled her with dread; altogether unnatural, that beast was. A strange thing.

Betsy's heel turned on the pavement, sending her tumbling to the ground. The piece of paper fluttered from her hand and tumbled cartwheels down the driveway. Her file on Mr. Desmond Rudder spilled from her hand, sending some papers aloft on the breeze as others stuck in the red paint.

"Shit!" she screamed, grabbing her ankle. It wasn't broken, but it was likely a bad sprain. What would Mr. Potter say if she had to request time off to see a doctor? One thing was for sure; she could write off any chance of him asking her out on a date. He only dated winners, not losers who fell down on the job. Damn!

Betsy grabbed the station wagon's side mirror and used it to pull herself to her feet. Her ankle held her weight but walking was painful, and her shoe was cracked at the heel. The bruising would be horrendous. As she walk-hopped in the direction of her car, there was another movement on her left; the elk had moved closer. It was only a few feet away now.

"Shoo!" she said, flapping her hands at it. "Get on out of here. Shoo!"

The elk lowered its head and laughed with the deep voice of a man.

"Wha…what!" Betsy screamed. The sound of the elk's laughter sliced through her mind; wrong, it was all wrong. Elk don't laugh. They don't…

It charged. Her ankle bent again on its broken heel and she leaned back on the station wagon for support, putting her hands up to fend off the elk, a useless gesture. It slammed its antlers into her body at her pelvis, pinning her to the station wagon, snapping bones. Her upper body was thrust forward over the elk's head, and for a moment she smelled its musty hair. The antlers were covered in the same red paint she had found on the front door, and reeked of rot. Fleas jumped on the animal's head and leaped onto her forearms, but she was unable to shake them off; her hands didn't work anymore. Nothing in her body seemed to work anymore. The elk pushed harder and harder, until the pressure on her belly threatened to burst her eyes from her head. But before they could pop she closed her eyelids, and felt much better. In her final seconds, she silently prayed that her new blue dress was not torn beyond repair.

CHAPTER 16 - The Wapiti of 1959

"**I**'m nervous. Oughtn't I be a little nervous? I'm going to be a mother, William."

"Of course, dear. It's perfectly natural."

Nancy sat on the edge of her favorite chair, the one covered in embroidered primrose vines. Her ankles were crossed, and her hands pressed on her kneecaps. "I only hope…"

"Everything will be wonderful, my dear," William said around the cigar bobbing between his lips. "The boy will love it here, I have no doubt about it at all."

The adoption agency van beeped twice at the bottom of the drive, announcing its arrival.

"He's here!" Nancy gasped. "What should I do? Do I look presentable?"

"You look lovely, my dear. The boy won't mind a bit."

"Mind what? What do you mean? Is it my hair?" Nancy dashed to the bathroom for a final look at the mirror.

The van crept up toward the house, navigating the tricky circular driveway with careful precision until it stopped in front of the door and beeped once more. William rose from his chair and tossed his newspaper on the coffee table. Nancy emerged from the bathroom to scoop it up and fold it, trying to keep the room tidy for the arrival of their adopted son. Everything must be perfect.

Someone rapped on the front door with a knuckle, and muffled voices chatted on the other side. William tugged on his jacket, slicked back his hair, and opened the door with a grand gesture that Nancy found embarrassing. She positioned herself behind him, ready to present a more measured demeanor to the boy as well as whoever had brought him.

The nurse was a youngish man in his late twenties, with center-parted hair and institution-green scrubs. He grinned and held out his hand for William to shake.

"You must be William Stubbs," the nurse said. "I'm Handey, Nurse Handey. It's a pleasure to meet you!"

"Likewise, Mr. Handey. Is that our Mickey, hiding behind you there?"

The boy was thinner than he should have been for ten years of age, but his cheeks were ruddy and his arms were strong. He scowled at William from behind the nurse, although his expression was one made more of nervousness than of belligerence.

"Come on out, my dear," Nancy said. She held out both her arms, hoping he would consent to a hug, but was disappointed. The boy shrank back further, hiding his face.

"Never mind that," Nurse Handey said. "Give him some time. You all got along pretty well when you met last month, didn't you?"

"Like gangbusters!" William said, grinning. "Don't ya remember me, Mickey?"

Mickey shook his head.

"Sure you do," Nancy said. "Anyway, come on in! Mickey, I'll show you right to your room, if you like. I had it all made up just for you. The agency said you like baseball. Is that right?"

Mickey nodded.

"Well then, just wait until you see it! Come and look. It's this way, just down the hall."

While Nancy showed Mickey his new room, the men sat in the living room. William poured two glasses of whiskey, and lit another cigar.

"Wow!" Nurse Handey said. "You got a whole arbore-tum going on in here, don't ya?"

"Nancy took up gardening a few years ago. Turned the house into a real jungle. I'm not fond of the clutter, myself, but she's crazy for it."

Nurse Handey gazed around the room at the hanging pots near the window, the clusters of ferns by the door, and a container of green moss and leafy sprouts on the glass table next to his chair. He nudged the container back a few inches to make enough room to set down his drink.

"Thanks for bringing him by," William said. "The wife's been in a total dither since we signed the papers. It's a relief to finally have the boy here."

"It's my job, sir," Nurse Handey said. "But I'm glad to do it. Better than the other side of it, you know. The picking-up jobs are a lot worse."

When Mickey and Nancy returned from his bedroom the boy had calmed. In his arms he gripped a teddy bear wearing a baseball cap.

Nancy smiled. "Mickey wants to say something to you, Nurse Handey."

The nurse handed his glass to William, and knelt in front of Mickey. "And what's that, my boy?"

"Thank you," Mickey said in a stuttering voice. "I am going to be okay now. My new room is real neat, and I like my new parents, too."

"Good!" the nurse said, smiling. "That's what I like to hear. Well, I'd better hit the road. Thank you for your hospitality, Mr. Stubbs, and congratulations to you both! Let us know if you have any problems. You can call us at any hour, and someone will pick up. You have the number written down?"

"Sure do," William said, offering his hand again. "Thanks again. You drive safe now, you hear?"

At dinner, Mickey said little between bites.

"Don't you like the food?" Nancy asked. She had been nervous about her cooking. Having never cared for a child before, her recipe book had been assembled with a more adult palate in mind. What did children like to eat? Hot dogs and ketchup, most likely, but she hoped she could provide better nutrition than that. She had prepared a casserole, with plenty of cheese. And there was vanilla ice cream for dessert.

Mickey nodded. "It's okay. Better than at the orphanage."

Nancy beamed.

"Do you like soda pop?" William asked.

She had known that was coming. William worked at the FizzPopCo factory as a junior director of production, and in addition to his paycheck he brought home a whole case of soda bottles every week.

Mickey nodded again. "It's my favorite thing in the whole world, other than baseball."

William grinned. "Of course it is! Well, you finish your dinner and we'll all have some pop with ice cream in it. It's called a float. Sound good to you?"

"I'm done," Mickey said. But his plate was still half full.

"Doesn't look like it to me," William said. "Why don't you eat a little more?"

"Shush, William. He's eaten plenty. Let's all go watch the television."

Mickey's eyes popped open wide. "You have a television?"

"Sure do!" Nancy grinned. "Have a seat in the living room, and I'll make us all some FizzPop floats."

Nancy discovered the soda bottle caddy in the refrigerator was empty. William never refilled it, the lazy ox. The cupboard was empty, too. He usually kept an extra crate of bottles in the back of his truck, so she stepped into her house slippers and put on her coat. The wind was blowing tonight.

Halfway to the truck, she noticed a splash of color in the driveway. The night was dark, but she could see that the color was red. It was wet, too. It looked a bit like blood.

Nancy frowned. Jasper, William's old retriever, had a bad habit of nabbing wild rabbits in the forest and leaving their gooey remains in the driveway like some kind of arcane offering. Awful old dog. She scanned for bits of fur, but found instead a scrap of fabric; hospital green, like Nurse Handey's scrubs. It was the exact same color, in fact.

Her feet went numb, and her knees wobbled. Just what, exactly, was a piece of Nurse Handey's uniform doing in a pool of rabbit blood? That didn't make a lick of sense.

Unless it wasn't rabbit blood.

Nancy's mind slowly turned the corner on the situation. If it wasn't rabbit blood, and Jasper was chained up at the back of the house like Nancy knew he was, then it might be Nurse Handey's blood. Of course, that didn't make much sense either.

Nancy looked up from the pool and glanced toward the forest. She had always suspected there was something out there that was dangerous. Not an animal, no; it was something far worse than any creature Mother Nature would set loose upon the world. Sometimes on warm summer evenings there would be a wild cry that didn't sound like any earthly animal, and all the other creatures would raise their voices in answer. Sometimes the ground had long scores dug into the mud. Worst of all were the little earthquakes, followed by the smell of smoke, but there had never been a fire. And how could there be smoke without fire?

The ground shook, and something caught her eye; two bright red coals sat high in the branches of the pines, smoldering. But when they moved, their motion was in unison, as if bound together. They were not coals, but eyes, and they watched her in the night. Down the pine tree they descended, then across the yard they charged, fixated on her.

Nancy screamed, and her legs stopped working. She fell to the driveway, landing in the sticky puddle, and felt something hard bruise her bottom. Her fear was not so great that she could ignore what was prodding her, but when she found it she was not relieved; it was a human hand. Nurse Handey's hand.

When Nancy came to, she was resting on the couch in her pajamas. William was in his chair, puffing on a cigar held in a trembling hand.

"What happened?" Nancy asked. "How did I get into my pajamas?"

"I changed you," William whispered. "Your dress was soiled." He sat in his favorite chair with his shotgun resting across his knees.

The memory of what had occurred in the front yard rushed back to her all at once. "William! The nurse, he…"

"I know. I already called the police."

"Did they come? Where are they?"

William frowned. "They're out front. They're…" he hesitated, then made a sound like a tiny sob stuck in his throat. "In pieces. Many pieces."

"Oh my god," Nancy said. Then, suddenly, "Mickey! Is he safe?"

"He's in his room. Didn't see a thing. Aim to keep it that way, too. He's a good boy, Nancy."

"Did you see it? What happened?"

William sighed, and stared at his cigar. "It was an elk. Either gone mad, or maybe rabid, although I've never heard of such a thing in deer. It got the nurse, I think, and then it got the cops who answered my call. Lived here for almost ten years, we have, and never seen anything like it. Never heard of such a thing." William's eyes drifted to the sliding door, and he gazed out at the forest. "Never."

"But how…"

"It's still out there, Nancy." William turned to her. "It's right outside the door." His voice quieted to a whisper, and tears streamed down his cheeks.

Nancy was terrified. She had never seen William frightened before. She had seen him drunk, haughty, proud, angry, and horny. But never, ever frightened.

A voice loud enough to rattle the windows boomed from the front stoop. "William Stubbs! You are bound to this house. You are bound to me!"

"Who on earth…" William started, but he did not move from his chair. He sat, with his feet rooted to the hardwood floor.

A shuddering wail of dread drifted out from the hallway. Mickey cried into his new pillow, on his new bed, stricken with fear. Nancy ran to the hallway, but when she tried his door she found it locked.

"Mickey? Open the door, my darling boy. Please."

The wailing grew louder, and dissolved into sobs. "Why are you doing this to me?" the boy screamed. "Who is outside? I don't want to go back!"

"We don't know, but we will protect you if you just…"

"No! Go away!"

The window was smashed inside the boy's room, and glass rained to the floor. Overturned furniture fell with thuds that shook the walls, and toys were crushed under stomping hooves. Seconds later, everything went quiet.

"Mickey?" Nancy screamed. "What happened?"

"Step aside," William said, before charging at the door with his shoulder. It broke open on his third try, as knob popped out from the wood in an explosion of splinters.

The boy was gone.

"Damn it!" William ran for the front door, grabbing his shotgun on his way.

"No! William!" Nancy tried to stop him, but he would not be deterred. He burst through the front door into the yard, whipping the barrel of his gun left, right, seeking a target at the tree line and finding none.

The elk, as well as whoever had been yelling from the doorstep, had left. Yet the yard was not empty, no; Mickey was still there. But he had been disassembled and reassembled, his limbs torn from his body before being laid on the ground in a tidy row at the side of his torso, like piglets at their mother's teats.

The driveway was a gruesome study in human anatomy. The sectioned bodies of the boy, the police, and the nurse had been accumulated and arranged in a display that conveyed a message Nancy could not decipher, all laid at perfect angles like ancient hieroglyphs.

She collapsed, and William knelt beside her, speechless, as his shotgun tumbled from his numb fingers.

And from the forest the elk stepped, blinking its diamond eyes.

CHAPTER 17

"D...Dad..."

Penny's teeth were chattering. She had always thought the saying was a figure of speech, but as adrenaline rushed through her body she could actually feel her front teeth clicking against each other.

She should have taken her father's warning more seriously. But she needed her notebook, and had misplaced it some time that afternoon. After searching the house for twenty minutes, she had remembered her notebook was on the little table on the back porch, next to Dad's stinky ashtray. After retrieving it, she had paused on the porch, stretching and breathing deep in the fresh air. The yard was out-of-bounds ever since they had tried to leave three days ago, and now that her acute terror of the elk was blunted by a couple of nights of sleep she could not resist enjoying the scent of the forest for a moment before going back into the house.

"Penny? What are you doing out there?" Her father was already calling her back inside. Of course she knew the porch was off limits, but how long could they be expected to hide from the elk-man? A week? A month? Forever?

Penny had turned her head to respond to her father, but what she saw at the end of the porch had almost made her drop her notebook.

A hare with glowing red eyes sat upright, with its forepaws resting on its belly. It was almost pure white but for the yellow stains and dry blood that streaked its fur. The tips of its ears were taller than Penny's head, and its feet were twice the length of her own. It did not charge her, as the elk had, but only stared at her with diamond eyes.

"Dad." Penny's voice was a low and raspy whisper, like it was in dreams when she wanted to cry for help but found she was unable to make a sound.

The hare's ears suddenly grew points all over—too many points, sprouting out from the flesh and expanding until they looked like antlers. Its front legs extended and its back legs straightened, and its fur turned into shredded scraps of dirty pelt that draped the body of a muscled man with a great rack of horns protruding from his head.

Penny wanted to start screaming in earnest then, but she was still unable to coax any noise from her throat. Her notebook fell to the deck and she tumbled backwards. Her feet tangled in the legs of her father's deck chair, and she fell hard on her hip.

The elk-man watched, but still did not attack. It only spoke to her. "Penny. I remember you. I remember your mother."

"You what?" Penny gasped.

"I met her in 1917. She had a heart of tree bark, that one. And eyes like burning coals."

Penny shook her head. Her mother had been born in 1944.

"Breasts like Mercury and Mars. Lopsided. Lop-eared."

Penny gripped her notebook in her hand and spider-walked backwards, seeking the edge of the deck. The elk-man seemed lost in thought, not especially interested in her. Maybe because she wasn't running. She had learned from a television show that running always excited predatory creatures. But now the other times he had whispered to her had all seemed like a dream, something that was hard to remember later; this time felt more real than ever before. It also felt more wrong.

"Look what I found," the elk-man said, noticing her again. He pried a gold bangle bracelet from his wrist and held it out to her. "Do you think it might be valuable?"

Penny slid under the railing and landed on her hands and knees in the dirt. She crawled, as fast as she could, until she was around the front corner of the house. The elk-man did not pursue, but only stood on the deck, holding out the bracelet in his hand with a lost look on his face.

Her father was sipping a drink in the living room when she burst through the front door, covered in dirt and pine needles, her face streaked with tears.

"D…" she managed to whisper, but her throat was still closed up.

"What happened?" He set his drink down but missed the table, and the glass tumbled to the floor. It had not been his first of the day.

"Ell…"

"El…elk? You saw the elk? Where?"

"Man." Penny pointed toward the back of the house.

Her father threw open the sliding door, but the creature was gone. On the patio table sat the bracelet he had offered to Penny. Her father picked it up and made a sour face, then threw it into the kitchen trash bin.

"Ugly thing," he muttered, as he retrieved his glass from the floor. "You okay, kiddo?"

Penny nodded. Her father had already checked out again. For the last few days, he had done little but sit in his fancy new chair and sip from his glass. It was like he had given up. Penny had seen him act like this before, years ago, when he was still hurting from his separation from Emily. She didn't know much about marriage, but she was old enough to understand what depression was and that her father suffered from it because he was a really wonderful man who just wanted everyone to be happy all the time. He even wanted Emily to be happy, even though they were divorced. That's why Penny loved him so much.

But he was not handling confinement well. When he had projects to do and there was a lot going on, it distracted him from his sadness. But now that they were locked in, trapped in the house all the time, he seemed dazed. Like he'd been hit on the head with a softball.

Penny decided it was up to her to save them both.

By midnight, Penny's voice had still not returned. When she tried to talk, her throat locked up, and her hands would shake. It felt like there was a tornado in her mind; a constant roaring of wind, blocking out her thoughts. The normal world was drifting away, and she was a ghost interacting with all the stuff from her old life. Only her bed still felt familiar, but she did not want to give up and lay down like Dad had done. Someone had to do something.

Through the wall, she could hear her father snoring in long, hitching breaths; snok-snok-snooork, whoosh.

She crept down the hall past his bedroom and made her way through the living room, keeping an eye on the sliding glass door for a pair of red glowing eyes peeking out from the darkness. After sneaking a soda from the refrigerator, she picked through the trash until a glint of gold shimmered among the waste; the bracelet.

It was very old. Spirals and cross-hatches were hand carved into the band. A round shape like a coin was mounted on the top, and fixed to it was a little sculpture carved in relief; a woman and a man wrapped around each other in an act of sex. The woman's eyes were hollowed-out holes, or maybe there used to be gems mounted in the sockets. The man had antlers protruding from his head, like those of an elk. It was the monster from the forest.

The bracelet was ugly, just like Dad had said. But it was precious, somehow, too. Utterly unique, and eons old. Whatever else it was, it was not junk. It did not belong in the kitchen trash can next to a rotting apple core and an empty oatmeal box. It was something to be cherished, even if it had belonged to the awful beast-man who had killed her precious Copper. She slipped it into the pocket of her robe. Now it belonged to her. She had taken something from him, and that made her feel good. The weight of it in her pocket made her wonder if it was real gold. It didn't seem like the cheap junk she and her friends sometimes bought at the mall. No, this was grown-up jewelry. The real deal.

She didn't bother tip-toeing on her way back to her room; Dad was snoring loud enough to wake the dead. After turning the lock on her door, she sat at her desk and opened her notebook. In the center, right in the exact middle of the book, was a page with a long vertical line drawn down the middle. On the left side she had written "Gleaner." On the right, she had written "Us." Gleaner had four points in his column; one each for the workmen, one for the collections lady, and one for Copper (this one had a tiny heart drawn next to it, to symbolize her own broken heart.) In the "Us" column she now added her first point; one for the bracelet. It might not be a person's life, like the others were, but it was something special, just as irreplace-able as a living being. She was sure of it.

Since her father had started being honest with her a few days ago, things had been both better and worse. It was good to know what was really going on. Having to make guesses and coming up with only the scariest answers was worse than knowing for sure, no matter how awful the truth was. Now that she knew what had happened to everyone, she started formulating plans; her notebook was filled with scribbles and drawings, schematics for useful devices, and escape routes. They couldn't fly out, that was obvious. Running out was no good, unless Gleaner could be distracted somehow—she was still working on that as a possibility. Digging out was a definite option, but Dad might think that was unrealistic. She wasn't so sure.

One of the biggest setbacks was that the phone line was out. Nothing but static for days, ever since they had tried to leave. The postman had stopped coming by, too. She had spent all day yesterday watching out the window, waiting for Mr. Samson to toddle past with his big bags, but he never showed up. Particularly strange was that she didn't see a single car drive by, either. And that seemed just about impossible. It was almost like there was some kind of haze at the property line, or a force field like something on Star Trek that separated the lot from the rest of the world.

Dad had shown her the little notes written by Desmond, but he had drawn the line at letting her poke her head down into the hatch. He wouldn't even move the sofa away from the wall. She thought Desmond didn't sound so bad, but Dad wasn't sure. There were even deeper levels below Desmond's, he said, which scared Penny badly, although she had tried not to show it.

Sitting at her desk, the soles of her feet tingled as though they felt a strange energy from the rooms below. How far down did they go? If there were two, there must be more. Maybe a lot more.

Penny flipped to a blank page and wrote at the top, "*Things We Know About Gleaner*".

1. He is a "mad old god" (???)
2. He is a man, a wapiti, and a giant
   rabbit. maybe other stuff too
3. The house is his house and it is a lot
   of houses all stacked on top of each
   other
4. He doesn't want anyone to leave or
   outsiders to visit

As she sat wracking her brain for anything else she might know about Gleaner, something squeaked against her bedroom window. The night outside was impenetrable; the new moon had plunged the forest into a darkness as thick as tar.

The squeak had sounded like a finger on wet glass, and she knew what she should do, but she was afraid to do it.

Her finger rested on the light switch for three whole minutes before she worked up the nerve to flick it off. As soon as she did, the drawing in the fog on the window was bright in the starlight; someone had traced a crude outline of a cat's head, a sad-face, and a flower.

Was Gleaner apologizing?

There were no red eyes in the forest, and no face peeking through the window. He had said what he had come to say, and left.

Against her better judgement, Penny was struck with pity for the creature. Maybe he hadn't meant to kill Copper. Maybe everything was just a big misunderstanding, after all.

CHAPTER 18

Clive, the absolute sweetheart, told Emily she could keep the truck for a few extra days as long as she promised to bring a full pan of her amazing brownies whenever she dropped it off.

Max's phone line had been dead for almost a week. More foreboding than that, she had an uneasy feeling in her gut, and her gut was always right. Something was wrong at 23 Old Mine Road. She was sure of it, sure as the stars in the sky.

Her plan had been to stay away from Max for a little while, maybe even a whole month. Long enough to see if Max would call her—which, if he did, would put her in control of what happened next. If Penny called instead, well that was even better. Emily would love to hear from her, but she didn't want to appear desperate. And so what if she was a little desperate? A mother should crave her child's voice, shouldn't she? It was only natural.

But that nagging in her gut never stopped, and she gave in to it only two weeks after she had left Max wanting more at his front door. She had called, and then called again, and then again—but each time, the line was busy.

For a while, she called every day. Then she called every few hours. Maybe Penny was chatting with a new girlfriend? Or maybe she had a boyfriend. She was getting close to that age, wasn't she?

But no. It was something else. And if it wasn't—if she drove all the way up there for nothing, and Max was displeased by her unannounced visit—then so be it. Her maternal instincts had never been strong, but today they were screaming at her.

Something was wronger than wrong.

The flat-roofed house and its lot looked much the same
as it had when she had left, except the station wagon had
scorch marks around the hood. The old junk heap had apparently caught fire. Luckily, nothing else had been burned
by the flames. The stacks of molded carpet were still there,
rotting in the summer heat. The lawn was worse than ever;
in fact, it now looked like it had been trampled by a herd
of buffalo. Max's utter disdain for home maintenance was
as strong as ever, it seemed.

She lingered in the truck's driver seat for an extra
minute to fix her face. If disaster awaited within the house,
whether it was of a social or more physical nature, she
would greet it with equanimity and perfect makeup. A
touch of blush on her cheeks to wipe away a few years, and
a swipe of mascara for the complete femme fatale look. A
hint of blue on the eyelids, a dash of glitter to draw the eye
away from the wrinkled corners. Eight years younger, like
magic. Bippity-boppity-boo.

After smooching her lips at the mirror one last time
and nodding in approval, she dumped her makeup into
her purse and slid down from the truck seat, landing in
the driveway on wobbly heels. Impossible to do that in a
ladylike way, but at least nobody had seen. Maybe if she
did well here today, she could still get that Mustang.

A scant odor of cold smoke wafted from the house—
or maybe the smell was from the burnt station wagon.
That seemed more likely. Still, the whole place reeked of an
eye-watering melange of mildew, mold, rot, and ash. And
there was another scent underneath it all; stale blood.

"Max?" She called his name as she walked toward
the door, trying to sound pleasant. When nothing stirred
in either the yard or the house, she tried again. "Penny?

Anyone home?"

"No!" Penny's voice was adamant, fierce. She didn't sound frightened, though. Worried, perhaps, or even dismayed.

"Penny? It's Mommy."

The girl burst through the front door, waving her arms. "You have to go! You have to go now! Before he comes back!"

"Who? Your father? I'm sure he wouldn't mind if..."

"No! Dammit, why are you here? Why now?"

Emily crossed her arms. "Well, I don't know! I thought you might be happy to see me. Where's your father? This place is turning into a real dump."

Max emerged from the house and stopped on the step with his hands on his hips. "Well. You've really done it this time, Emily."

"What the heck is everyone talking about?" Emily shouted. "What's the big deal? Your phone is out, you know! If you didn't have money for the bill, you should have at least told me, or sent a letter. I've been worried sick!"

Emily's daughter and ex-husband exchanged a look she found impossible to decipher. Worry, pity, condescension.

"Someone talk, and I mean right now! Or I'll leave and you'll never see me again. Is that what you want?"

Max's eyes darted toward the trampled lawn, then toward the forest. Whatever he was afraid of was not there; the day was still and hot, a typical mid-June afternoon.

"Dad, we need to get her inside," Penny said. "And then we are going to have to tell her. She shouldn't try to leave without knowing the risk."

"Risk?" Emily said. "Is this some kind of joke? I don't appreciate..."

"Everyone inside," Max said, stepping aside and holding the door wide open. "And we'll have a talk."

Emily could not stop shaking her head. No, no, and no. Nothing Max and Penny told her made sense. She had half decided she was the butt of a prank, or perhaps an unwitting contestant on one of those gag shows with the hidden cameras. But they sat together for an hour, talking about an evil being that lived in the forest, and no production crew popped out of the shadows. And something tickled at the back of her mind; she had seen a strange creature on the night she and Max had gone into the forest. An elk had appeared while they were on the forest floor, and it had damaged eyes, like some kind of mutation. Creepy, to be sure, but it was just an elk. The forest was full of them. Its behavior had seemed strange, but that didn't make it a demon or whatever Max and Penny were going on about. Yet they were adamant, and clear-eyed. Either they had lost their minds, or they were telling the truth.

Or what they thought was the truth.

"Tell you what," she said, "I'll just try to leave. I'll get in the truck and go, and if I make it out—which I will, I assure you—then we can put all this silliness to bed, and never speak of it again. Right?"

"You won't make it," Max said.

"Max, you're a grown man. Stop talking like that. You're scaring Penny."

"No he's not," Penny said.

"Anyway, you're both being ridiculous, and I don't believe a word of it. If you didn't want me here, you should have just said so, and saved us all a lot of time."

"Listen to us, Em," Max whispered. "If you're wrong, you're dead."

Emily scowled at him. "We'll see."

She shouldered her purse and hugged Penny. "I'm going to go now. I'll come back in a day or two. Then we'll see what's wrong with your phone, and go from there. It's clear you both need my help right now."

Max shrugged.

As confident as she was of her own safety, she could not resist hesitating for a minute on the front step to look around. But nothing moved, the yard was peaceful, and the forest was calm. Max and Penny stood tense behind her, staring out in wild-eyed terror at the breezy summer day. Emily looked back and smiled at them over her shoulder, trying to appear reassuring.

"I haven't said it often enough over the years, but hey…I love you both. I really do."

"We love you too, Mom," Penny said, but the expression on her face never changed, even during the brief moment when her gaze left the tree line.

Emily faced forward again so Penny couldn't see how big her grin was. It was a silly, loopy grin, filled with relief and joy. Penny still loved her! After everything, her girl still had room for her in her heart.

Halfway to the truck, Emily stopped and looked around again. The yard was still calm. She turned back toward Max and Emily and shrugged: *See? It's all good.*

The force with which the antlers struck her shoulder lifted her off her feet and propelled her over the top of the station wagon. She hit the roof hard, rolled over the hood and landed on her face on the driveway, spitting out teeth. Hooves stampeded around the trunk of the car and headed toward her again for another pass. Before the elk could trample her, she slid underneath the station wagon, pulling her body across the asphalt with her one unbroken arm.

Penny was screaming unintelligible words. Max ran

inside the house for something; a weapon? He didn't own a gun, didn't believe in them. Maybe he was just running away, like he always did.

The elk shrieked with rage and butted its antlers against the station wagon, rocking it back and forth. Laying on her back with the car's greasy innards directly above, Emily could only see its hooves—and then they were not hooves but human feet, darkened with mud, ankles wrapped in tattered skins lashed with leather straps. One foot slid back and a knee knelt down onto the hot pavement, and a hand reached underneath the car, grabbing her broken shoulder. The shattered bones grated together, grinding each other into splinters as he dragged her out toward the light. When she screamed in agony, one of her loosened teeth worked itself free of the gum and fell into the back of her throat, its sharp edges scraping as it went.

She was forced to swallow the tooth, before she could scream again, and again, and again.

CHAPTER 19

Max didn't understand much about what was going on, but he knew one thing: Penny wasn't going into the hatch with him, no matter how insistent she was.

Of course, once he was a level or two down, he didn't know how he could stop her from following. The hatch didn't have a lock inside. And he knew she wanted to meet Desmond, for some reason. She had a twisted idea that he might be an ally, or even a friend. Max knew better, though. Desmond might be harmless, but he was terrified of Gleaner beyond reason, and that alone made him dangerous.

He packed extra batteries for the flashlight, a bottle of water, the hammer he had grabbed while Emily was being attacked—it had proven to be a futile gesture, as Gleaner had already pulverized her by the time Max returned to the front door—and, for reasons he could not have explained, a rope. It was not a cave he was descending, but a house. Yet it still felt like he was about to go spelunking.

"I don't know how long I'll be gone. But I'm begging you, Penny, please don't follow me. If you love me, stay here. Please."

Penny frowned, but nodded. "Okay. I guess."

"Not good enough." Max knelt on the floor before his daughter, took her shoulders in his hands, and looked into her eyes. "You promise me you'll stay here. Don't even open the hatch to look down, no matter what. You hear me? I want you to promise."

She hesitated. As Max had suspected, she had clearly planned to sneak down after he had gone deeper. He did not let go of her shoulders until she sighed, and slumped with resignation. "Fine. I promise. Cross my heart, hope to die."

Max nodded, and tightened his belt. "All right. In his note, Desmond said the only way out is down. I'm going to find out exactly what that means."

"Dad, please be careful. I'm scared."

"Me too. But I think this part has to happen. Don't you?"

Penny nodded.

Max passed swiftly through Desmond's ashy living room, casting only a cursory glance toward the burned man rocking in his chair. He nodded and Desmond nodded back with the curt civility of city neighbors. Max tried to suppress the dissociation that arose in his mind in reaction to this casual relationship with a moving corpse; now would not be a good time to start freaking out. He had a long way to go.

When he asked the couple on the next floor down where their hatch was, they were reluctant to say. Their fear of Gleaner ran deep. Max found the little door on his own, holding his nose while casting around the room with the flashlight. It was under an end table, which crumbled into a mushy paste under his fingers as he tried to pull it off the hatch. Shoving the mess aside, he grasped the handle, which was fashioned from an embedded railroad spike. Holding his breath, he threw it open.

No ladder to climb down, this time; only an ancient rope tied to a wrought iron hook at the top, snaking down into the darkness. As he paused near the opening, steeling himself to descend, a cold hand settled on his shoulder.

"You don't have to, you know," the woman said. "Just go on back to your own home, and wait. All of this won't matter in the end. It never does."

Max shrugged off her clammy fingers and knelt, wrapping the rope around his hand. His upper body strength wasn't exactly tip-top. It would be a small miracle if he made it down to the next floor without twisting an ankle, or worse. But no answers remained in the rooms above; the only way forward was down.

He eased himself into the opening and gripped the rope between his knees. It chafed against his jeans, burning rough marks into the fabric as he slid down to the next floor.

The stench was overwhelming, a morning-after blend of bile and stale alcohol. Even before he could shine his light onto the room, he sensed a press of soft bodies, whispering, ogling him. In singles and pairs they crowded in the room, holding dust-coated wine glasses and pinching desiccated cigarettes between their bony fingers. Every face in the room had turned to watch his clumsy descent.

A skeletal body pressed itself against his back. In his ear, a ghost's voice whispered something about penetration, agony, and pleasure. Its abstract suggestions rode in on a waft of breath that was tangy with active decay. Max retched and stepped away, but collided with another party-goer. This one was nude, displaying a clear view of yards of loose skin draped over veins gone hard with clotted blood. Tangled in its wiry chest hair was an assortment of powdered bone, fingernails, and broken shards of teeth. It gestured toward its flaccid penis and smiled, stretching back its cheeks to reveal a row of teeth the color of rotten olives.

Every direction Max turned, he found another interested partygoer. When they spoke with their broken mouths, their words were delivered directly to his brain; he heard their soft statements, but no specific syllables could be picked up by his ears. A slithering whisper and the clicking of teeth conveyed a sense of desperation, hunger, and lust.

The light of his flashlight revealed colorful banners strung between the walls, festooned with cobwebs and roots. Dozens of glass bottles were collected on every surface, far too many for a simple soirée. But this party had been going on for decades. Max recognized the era. This room had been furnished in the 1940s. The decor filled him with uneasy nostalgia for his childhood home.

"Where's the hatch?" he said out loud, but the sound of his crude voice was overwhelming in the sordid den. The guests were unfazed, but the host stepped forward through the crowd. He wore a tuxedo and top hat, and a dried carnation poked from his lapel, paired with a twin-peaked pocket square.

"Stay," the host whispered. "Drink." His haunted eyes were coated in a white film, through which tiny bed bugs traced snowy trails in the inflamed sclera.

A skeletal guest wrapped her hand around Max's ankle. Another clawed at his thigh. They descended upon him with aching greed, petting him, begging.

"Drink with us," the host insisted, offering a bottle of tequila which housed a floating tarantula. Slender tendrils of decay floated around the spider like white hairs suspended in the liquid.

"Talk to us," one of the women whispered.

"Fuck us," one of the men pleaded.

Max tore his body free of the clambering guests and looked around the room for the next hatch, but the floor was covered in broken glass, party streamers, discarded plates, and shreds of cast-off clothing. He shuffled through the debris, but the hatch appeared to be buried. Twenty guests turned into thirty, then forty, as more shuffled out from the hallway in various states of undress. Even more

poured from the bedrooms, some missing limbs, others
wearing elaborate sex devices Max could not begin to
guess the purpose of. They threw themselves at his feet,
pressed him with their bodies until he was in danger of
being smothered.

Gagging in the stench, he thrashed free of their
grasping arms, ripping their delicate limbs from their
bodies. After disentangling their fingers and hands from
his clothing, he charged for the rope, praying under his
breath that he had the physical strength to climb it. It was
a feat he had never accomplished in junior high gym class,
but propelled by terror and disgust he managed to haul
himself high enough up the rope to grip the edge of the
upper floor and kick his way up through the hatch.

He slammed it shut behind himself, gasping. The
spore-laden air of the rotting couple's home smelled almost fresh after his visit to the eternal party below.

"Did you find what you were looking for?" the man
asked.

Max shook his head. He had not gone deep enough.
With his hands on his knees, he breathed hard, coughing
in the thick air.

"Rest for a minute," the woman said. "Come, have
a chat with Mickey. It will take your mind off things. It
always does for me."

"No," Max huffed. "I have to try again."

Without giving himself a chance to change his mind,
he descended the rope for a second time. The party guests
crushed in on him immediately, but he shoved them
back, grimacing as their frail bodies crumbled under his
strength. Striding through the living room, he kicked
empty bottles aside, laying the floor bare in his search for
the hatch. But there was none. Could he have arrived at
the lowest level? It seemed unlikely. Grim as this place

was, it was no lair for an old god.

When he reached the hallway, he balked. Naked body
parts lined his path. Small dried rivers of fluids pooled
from the doorways in layers of color; brown, white, bur-
gundy. Clenching his jaw, he stepped forward. His boots
stuck to the floor and peeled up with every step.

A quick glance into the room which lay directly under
his own small bedroom told him the hatch was not there.
The floor was bare, but bodies in various states of decay
and undress hung from the ceiling on chains and hooks.
He moved along with his eyes averted until he met with
the door which would be his daughter's, in his own house.
Fighting his reluctance—it was not really Penny's room,
after all—he pushed the door open with the end of his
flashlight.

Directly in the center of the room was the hatch.
It was white, constructed of bones lashed together with
strips of dried tendon. On all sides lay the draping bodies
of spent partygoers, writhing in pain and ecstasy, but there
was something wrong with those bodies—they had been
taken apart, then reconstructed. A torso with four arms
and three legs embraced a two-headed creation which balanced on one leg with two feet. Each corner of the room
held a pile of parts, but the pieces were stitched together in
ways both right and wrong, the psychotic handiwork of a
party host who had been locked in with his guests for too
many long years.

"Do you like my work?" The host stood behind Max
in the hallway, holding his hat in his hand. "They are all
quite happy, you know. I've made sure of it. You could join
them."

Max reached the hatch in three steps and yanked on
the handle. To his relief, he found a sturdy ladder down
to the next level. It appeared to be made of bone, but such

details did not bother him now. He was becoming numb
to the horrors of the stack.

The floor of the level below tickled at his ankles. It was
thick with fur, three feet deep. Mites crawled through it,
an entire civilization of gnawing insects. Max found no
furniture in the light of his flashlight, and no residents.
The room was empty, with only brown walls and layers
upon layers of mangy brown hair.

"Hello?" he whispered, hoping he would receive no
response. When no one answered, he shuffled his feet
through the hair, seeking the next hatch. His toe struck
something hard; a bone, which rattled across the floor
under the hair when kicked. Was it from the party above,
or had it originated here on this level?

In the kitchen, Max found two skeletons, their bones
gouged by the gnawing teeth of an animal. The remains
did not speak to him, which came as yet another relief.

Finding no hatch in the kitchen, he moved on to the
entryway near the front door. As with all the other levels,
dirt pressed up against the glass windows, and the front
door was securely sealed. Pestilential hair was heaped up
against the door in a mound four feet deep. Every time the
piles moved, clouds of choking hair drifted into the air.

From somewhere down the hallway—the room that
mirrored his own—came a deep growl. It was an enormous sound, rumbling and sick, angry and hungry. The
floorboards creaked under its weight as the animal rose to
its feet and moved into the hallway. Before it turned the
corner to the living room, Max clicked off the flashlight
and huddled behind a mound of infested hair, his skin
twitching with fear and disgust.

The creature was a dog. Max recognized the breed as
a mastiff, with great drooping ears and sad eyes. It stalked

down the hallway, moving slowly until it sensed Max over the overwhelming scent of decades of its own shed hair. It stopped with its nose up in the air, breathing heavily.

Max cowered in the corner by the door as tiny bugs crawled up his ankles into his pant legs. They started to bite; not just mites, but fleas as well, stinging his skin, a hundred pin pricks. He bit his tongue hard enough to draw blood, holding back a groan of pain.

The mastiff shook its loose pelt, and in the dim light shining through the floorboards overhead Max saw a tornado of hair puff into the air and settle again on top of the accumulated piles. Loose hairs drifted into his eyes, stuck to his cheeks, tickled his nose. The dog's interest in Max's presence waned, and it lay down to lick the hair from the bottom of its pads with a massive tongue. After several minutes of cleaning, the mastiff finally moved into the kitchen and settled on the floor. Crunching and slurping, it gnawed on the bones of the house's previous residents.

Max crawled toward the hallway, searching the wooden floorboards with his hands, pushing rolling mounds of hair ahead as he went. The mastiff raised its head, dropping a bone that clattered to the kitchen floor. It was no use; the dog's hearing was too sharp. He had no chance of exploring this level undetected.

Max sprinted for the bone ladder. He skipped rungs two by two, slamming the hatch open above his head.

Through the party he ran, ducking the reaching hands of the propositioning guests. Up he dashed through the rotting living room, ignoring Mickey's mushy parents. Desmond was not in his rocking chair when Max passed through his room, which suited him just fine. He emerged finally in his home with shaking hands, coughing dog hair from his lungs.

"Penny," he gasped. "I'm back. I'm okay."

There was no answer. Max threw open the front door, and slammed open the back slider. He bolted down the hall to check Penny's bedroom, but it was empty. Max's own was untouched, and the workroom was as he had left it. Every door in the house was open, except for the hatch.

But Penny was gone.

CHAPTER 20 – The Wapiti of 1949

"So very avant-garde, Luis. How horrifically *rustic* it all is!"

The woman crooning in Luis's ear was new to the industry and overly desperate to please, but she had the spark. A real "it" girl. She had a big future in front of her—if she lived through the early years, of course. If she could handle Hollywood at its meanest. The woman might even be a star, if she kept her nose clean. If, if, if.

He kissed her gloved hand, and winked. "Isn't it? This place is my sanctuary. I've been coming up here to write for nearly a decade now. I wrote *Autumn's Mist* at that very desk, over in the corner there." He gestured toward his well-oiled rolltop that looked out over the forest through the sliding glass door.

"No!" the woman gasped. "Really? I loved that one! I saw that picture in the theater when I was only nine years old!"

"Hush, now," Luis demurred. "You age me horribly with your words."

The woman paled. "Oh, Luis! I'm so sorry! I didn't mean to…"

"Nonsense. I'm only teasing you, darling. Here, have a tequila, on me," Luis winked again, letting her off the hook.

He had rarely invited outsiders to his private forest home in times past, but during the winter of 1948 he had developed a keen interest in astrology. A silly hobby, perhaps, but he thought he might write a script based on a fortune teller who fell in love with a lion tamer. It would be no great masterpiece, of course, but an end-of-summer romance with just a bit of quirk would set the tone for the new decade. Audiences would gobble it up.

The costume party was a nod to his new hobby; a real pagan midsummer celebration. He wanted to greet the season with plenty of guests, enough people to pack the little house—and enough drink to keep them entertained until the clock struck midnight. As he had anticipated, despite the distance from Los Angeles the party was a smash hit.

The dancers he had hired were dressed in green leaf bikinis. They undulated under warm spotlights, giving the glitter on their skin a watery effect. The guests had arrived wearing pointed ears like forest elves, flower-print dresses, island leis, and princess gowns. They took a cue from the dancers and moved closer to each other, dancing among the bikini girls with hands on hips and lips on lips. The soirée was fresh, healthy, joyous. Just the right mood for his new script.

"Luis! Over here!" A woman beckoned him. She was Madame Ivy—not her real name, but one she had donned for the occasion. Everyone knew the aging starlet's true name, of course, but Luis's parties were meant to bring whimsy to the otherwise dull lives of the Hollywood elite. It was lonely at the top, and a bore. Everyone needed a night off from themselves, sometimes.

"Coming, my darling Ivy. But let me just refill my drink first."

"I'll do that for you." A slender young man with slicked hair and greedy eyes pressed his hip against Luis as he refilled his glass. Before the man broke their physical connection, he tilted his head to one side and ran his fingers down Luis's spine. An invitation for later, undoubtedly. Luis nodded, a wordless agreement. He would find him in the back room, as soon as Madame Ivy was taken care of.

"Luis?" Madame Ivy called again from the back of the crowd. "Where did you run off to?"

"Coming!" Luis made his way through the guests, enduring worshipful glances and kowtowing bows from blossoming young producers. The industry never slept. Even at a casual party such as this, the ass-kissing never ended. Luis didn't mind. Their deference told him he was still at the top of his game. When such annoyances ended, he would know the open door to his public life was beginning to close, and it was time to step back into the shadows. Perhaps when it did, he would move up to this little house permanently. Something about the place had always called to him.

He found Madame Ivy with a handsome gentleman at her side. They were dressed in complementary costumes; Hermia and Robin Goodfellow from *A Midsummer Night's Dream*.

"There you are!" Madame Ivy gushed. "I would like to introduce you to my lovely cousin. Gina, say hello to Luis, my darling child. He's Hollywood's top film producer, and a fabulous writer as well." She grinned at Luis over her drink as he walked into her trap.

Gina was a gawky, gangly thing. Her flesh was too scant for pictures, and her frame was too bent for additional weight to hang right on the bones anyway. A hunch in her upper back at so young an age would never be rectified. She wore a costume that Luis assumed was meant to resemble a mermaid; an unflattering flesh-tone top with a tattered green corset, paired with a sequin skirt studded with limp bunches of satin seaweed and tufts of taffeta. She was an irredeemable mess suitable only for television, or perhaps the stage if she was lucky. Of course, it would never do to say such things to Madame Ivy, who clearly

intended to land the girl a role in one of his own movies.
She should have known better.

"How delightful to meet you, Gina," Luis said, bowing
before the girl. As he did, tequila spilled from the lip of his
glass. And so there was yet another blow against the waif;
she had made him spill his drink.

The girl curtseyed—*curtseyed*, for god's sake!—and
blushed, unable to speak in a fit of anxiety.

Luis sneered. "Well. I truly hope the two of your enjoy
the rest of the party. Your costumes are quite interesting.
And it's so nice to see you in particular, Madame Ivy, but
I believe I hear someone in the back guest room is calling
my name and so I must move along now."

"You're such a good host," Madame Ivy oozed.
"Please, don't let us keep you."

"I won't."

Luis nodded to a portly director as he passed by the
entryway—a fresh import from France and a little too
haughty for his own good, but talented—and moved on
down the hall. The first bedroom was gussied up as an
opium den, just as a lark. Luis had ordered it specially
decorated for the occasion, enlisting the help of a designer
from Italy who happened to be in San Francisco for an
art show. Swags of fabric were hung from the ceiling, and
the floor was obscured by dozens of silk pillows. The odor
wafting down the hall was intoxicating, but not strong
enough to cause the swooning effect which nearly swept
Luis off his feet.

An earthquake shook the house. Wine glasses jangled
against each other in the cabinet, and the house creaked
as it rocked. Some of the guests laughed, believing it to
be an elaborate party trick played by their host. Luis was
not laughing. The effect was not his doing, and he did not
appreciate the interruption.

He returned to the entryway to address his guests. Raising his glass and his voice, he commanded their attention in his best director tone. "To those of you who are California natives, we are merely experiencing a little reminder that you have not left your homeland, despite the scenic drive you embarked upon to get here." His joke produced giggles from the crowd, as he had anticipated it would.

"To those of you new to the region, please feel free to panic, so that we may take photographs of your discomfort to use in future blackmail endeavors," he quipped. Another round of titters from the guests, but more uneasy this time. The rolling motion had not yet stopped.

In fact, the shaking was intensifying. A guest in an elf costume tried the front door, but it was locked. He issued a high, tinny scream, wrenching the knob with white-knuckled hands. "You can't lock us in! This isn't funny, Luis! You let us out right now!"

Luis's awards case toppled, adding more mess to the broken shards of bottle glass which littered the floor. Several guests panicked and rushed for the sliding door to the back porch, but it was sealed as tight as the front. They turned toward him, snarling with anger.

"Let us out immediately! Is this some kind of joke? A sick prank? You've taken this too far, Luis."

"I assure you…"

Before Luis could finish his protestation, the house lurched, and for a second the floor left Luis's feet. The entire building was sinking, rumbling as it descended into the earth. Dirt crept up the sliding glass door and the front windows, gradually blocking the view of the forest and the circular driveway.

Guests screamed, finally losing their equanimity as the outside world disappeared. Luis dashed down the hall toward the master bedroom, seeking to escape through the window there, but by the time he reached it the room was already underground. In minutes, the only remaining light in the house came from an assortment of cigarette lighters gripped in the trembling hands of Luis's angry guests.

"Where did he go?" someone shouted. "He's hiding! We have to find him!"

The crowd was becoming ugly in its fear. Luis ducked into the closet, knowing they would eventually find him. For the first time in his manicured, privileged life, he felt truly frightened.

The mob checked the kitchen, then the guest room. When they threw open the door to the master bedroom, Luis's heart pounded in his chest. They had all gone mad, lost their minds to a mixture of terror and booze and the unfamiliar sensation of powerlessness.

In moments, they had discovered him and dragged him out from the closet. He looked around at his guests, a scared throng of affronted elite holding up their lighters like pitchforks and torches, and laughed.

"What do you think you're doing, my dear friends? Something strange has happened, to be sure. But it is my solemn vow to you that it was not of my doing. And surely the party does not have to end here? Let's all have another drink, shall we?"

"I demand that you call me a cab, this instant!"

"And I as well! We're getting out of here!"

"Of course," Luis said. "Not a problem. There is a hatch in the ceiling in the living room that leads to the roof. I never had a use for it before, but I believe it will serve us well now. Shall we all go find it together?"

The crowd, calming, followed him to the living room. Some had even poured fresh drinks for themselves during the wait; it seemed that gentility had prevailed.

"There it is," Luis said, pointing at the upper hatch. "Who is hale enough to open it without a ladder?"

"I'll do it." The speaker was the young man who had solicited him earlier. And, Luis vowed, a young man who would see a starring role in one of his future movies.

"Give him a boost," Luis told a stodgy investor.

The two men struggled under the hatch for a minute or two until it was finally thrown open, and the guests sighed collectively at the sight of the bright, starlit sky overhead. The young man hoisted himself up through the hole and sat at the edge for a moment before pulling his feet the rest of the way through.

"Now, who's next?" Luis asked the group. Hands shot up.

Before another guest could ascend, the young man screamed. It was such a horrendous scream, so filled with wrenching dread and madness that for a moment Luis almost couldn't place the sound. The thunderous trampling of a hundred hooves shook the roof, as if Old Saint Nick had arrived on his Christmas route via Hell itself, and the young man's body tumbled down through the hatch opening.

It was in pieces, torn asunder by a relentless force. Mangled chunks of the poor youth were held together only by the remains of his tuxedo. His face was missing from its skull, which was, perhaps, a blessing, if the scream he had uttered was any indication of his mood in his final moments.

"Well," Luis said, offering his guests a manic smile. "We won't be leaving that way, now, will we?"

The partygoers looked at each other with the dazed stare that accompanies deep shock. Luis gathered as much of their attention as he could muster, and smiled again. He had always taken pride in his genteel composure. It was what had paved the way for him in Hollywood, and had opened doors and legs over the course of his long career. And he saw no reason he should quit that now. So, here was the million dollar question: What would the world-famous producer and screenwriter, Luis Alonzo III, do now?

He would keep his guests calm, wait out the problem, and have a lovely time doing so. And maybe have a nice fuck in the back room while he was at it. That's what he would do.

"Well, now. I'm sure this will all sort itself out. It's not as if the whole world is going to forget a room full of famous people, is it? They'll come looking for us right away, I have no doubt."

The guests nodded, relaxing. That all made perfect sense.

"In the meantime," Luis said, flashing a cool grin, "Who wants another drink?"

Hands shot up.

CHAPTER 21

Max returned to his senses with the telephone receiver clenched in his hand. It creaked under the fury of his grip, ready to split.

He remembered screaming into the hissing static on the line, something about bringing Penny back. In a high, desperate voice, he threatened Mr. Puck, Gleaner, and anyone else who could hear him on the other end of the dead line. In the back of his mind, behind the wall of rage, he knew it was a pointless outburst. But the phone was his only connection to the entity which owned the house, other than simply striding out into the wild forest.

And that was the only remaining option, wasn't it? He would have to march out to meet his enemy, since his enemy would not come to him. Penny was not in the house, and if she had disobeyed him to descend into the levels below he would have passed her during his rush back up to the top. He would have seen her. So, she had to be somewhere outside the house, which meant she was in danger from Gleaner. Or maybe she was already…

Max slammed the phone into its cradle and pulled a kitchen knife from the rack. It would be little use against the elk or the man, but if the hare showed up, he thought he could do it some damage.

He stormed into the back yard, his face frozen into the grimace of a young soldier rushing headlong into his first battle. Down the back steps he staggered, slipping on old pine needles and nearly putting the knife in his own face before catching his balance on the rail. The forest was undisturbed, the mangled fence no more or less broken than ever. There was no sign of Penny, and no indication of disturbance. Except for the treehouse…it was aglow.

Someone had lit it on fire. Tiny screams issued from inside which made Max's heart leap, but they were not a girl's screams. The wet wood was warping, hissing in the heat. It squealed as steam escaped its fibers. Penny's parade of painted figures on the side panels faded first to sepia tones, then to black as the fire licked them up.

The tree would catch soon, and then the forest. And the house.

Max scrambled for a hose, and managed to douse the flames before they could creep up the trunk into the upper boughs. Had Gleaner set the fire? He must have, but it seemed odd that he would endanger the house he was so protective of.

Then again, Gleaner was a mad old god, and rarely did his actions make sense.

"Ahh, it was such a pretty little fire, though," a voice rasped beside him. Desmond stood on the porch, swaying, watching smoke billow from the remains of the treehouse. "Too bad you put it out."

"Did you set it?"

"Not I. It must have been the G-man. He's a wild card, that one."

For the first time, Desmond's body was visible to Max in full light. The extent of his burns was far beyond anything that might have been survivable; the fire had gutted him, eaten his stomach, his eyes, all his soft tissue. Ashy bones poked through wherever the flesh was missing.

"You aren't supposed to be up here, Desmond. Go home."

"I wanted to talk to you. About your girl."

"Do you know where she is? If you do, tell me. No games."

"She's down below. Deep. Real deep." The burned man

started to sway again, humming under his breath.

"What did you see? Please, Desmond. Please help me find her."

"Didn't see a thing, but I heard a scrabbling sound. Is that a word? The G-man can dig like the dickens, you know. He scrabbled down right past my front windows. Just a few feet out, in the dirt. Down, down, down, and where he stops nobody knows. Maybe all the way at the bottom. Here's the really crazy part, though; he had someone else with him. I know that 'cause I could hear screaming. The G-man never screams. He's cool as a cucumber." Desmond grinned. "I hate him."

"Did it sound like a girl? Like Penny?"

"Mighta been. Who else could it be?"

"No one."

Max sunk into his patio chair. So, Gleaner could dig. Obviously, Max couldn't do anything like that. Penny had been taken, and he couldn't do a damn thing about it. But at least Desmond seemed to think she was alive; that was something.

"Here." Desmond offered Max one of his own cigarettes, and lit another for himself. They sat together, smoking on the patio, listening to the whispering silence of the forest.

Max's hands shook as he struggled to keep his grip on his cigarette. "What do I do, Desmond?"

The burned man inhaled, taking a deep drag, smiling with pleasure. Smoke puffed out between each rib, drifting from the open chest cavity where his lungs used to be. He looked like an anti-smoking commercial that aired on television during the after-school shows.

"You can't stop the stack from collapsing, and you can't get away, so far as I can tell. But you should probably try to get her back anyway. The place where the G-man took her, it's…" Desmond frowned. "It's pretty bad."

Max's heart pounded. Oh, Penny. He had not protected her. He had been too weak, or too stupid. "Tell me about the stack. Why does it collapse?"

"The G-man does it every ten years, at midnight on Midsummer's Day. Think he can only work up that level of power about once a decade. The closer we get to collapse, the stronger he gets. Maybe in ancient times he used to be even stronger, but he's getting up in years. Anyway, whoever is inside the stack at the time goes down with it, and they die. But they don't exactly stop living, you know? They keep on keepin' on, even though they're dead. Then G-man makes a new house appear in the lot, in just a few hours. Before sunrise, a new trap is set and the bait is laid, all ready for someone to move in and start the whole thing over again. It's an odd thing, and that's about all I understand."

"On the level below yours, there's a couple with a son who's in pretty bad shape."

"Ah, that's Mickey. Poor kid. He died before the stack collapsed, but it was close enough to midsummer that he was trapped too. The timing matters, somehow. G-man was strong enough to catch him up and keep him close, even without the collapse."

"So he's still conscious? In that dismembered state? That's horrible."

Desmond nodded. "Yup, wouldn't surprise me if he was. Here's the thing, though, Max. The G-man, he's not sane. I don't know why he does it, and I'm not sure he even remembers anymore either. He keeps some people, but not all. The lucky ones just die. The world has moved on, but the G-man's thousands of years old, some kind of leftover from the olden days. I think maybe he's dying. People don't worship the archaic gods of the land anymore, so he goes out and gathers them instead. They don't come to give him offerings, so he draws them in, and then he keeps the ones he likes best. He collects them."

"But Penny and I have only been living here for a few months, not ten years."

"You were a replacement. The ones who were here before you, up 'til the winter of '78, he took a dislike to. He decided not to keep them. They're dead now, and I mean proper dead. Not like me. I think he…you know, sees un-death as his gift to the ones he likes. The previous residents on your level didn't deserve his favor. Get it?"

"Not really."

"Well, that's all I got for you. I don't get out much these days, you know." Desmond grinned, sending puffs of smoke through the holes in his gaping cheeks.

"And the ones below you in the stack, Mickey and his parents…"

"We don't talk much, anymore. Did a bit at first, but it's best to keep your neighbors at arm's length, don't you know? 'Specially when you can't move away. Anyway, you'll get used to it."

"No I won't. I'm going to find Penny, and we're going to get out of here."

Desmond chuckled. "It's never happened, Max. He's never let a resident go, once he decided to keep them."

Max crushed his cigarette in the ashtray. "Well, it's going to happen this time. I don't care much about me, but if Penny is alive, I will find her. So either help me out, Desmond, or stay the fuck out of my way."

Desmond shrugged. "Penny's alive. He seems to like her, and it's not midsummer yet so there's probably still time. But I've no idea how you'll get to her unless you go all the way down the stack, and that's suicide. I'd do more if I could, but I've told you all I know, and this old body is barely sticking together enough to get me back down the old ladder to my own little estate. Not sure how much help I'd be to you. Anyway…" He dropped his voice to a whisper. "The G-man, he's not sane, you know. Not sane, not sane, not sane at all. He terrifies me."

Max found the place in the front yard where Gleaner had dug into the earth. The ground there was disrupted, dirt clods thrown aside to create a sunken navel where he had descended with Penny into the bowels of Hell. Gleaner did not arrive to attack Max as he inspected the yard; he probably knew Max could never leave without Penny, so he didn't bother. Max also suspected Gleaner was not very interested in him, in general. His sights had been set on Penny all along, and with her abduction he had nearly fulfilled his main purpose in this ten-year cycle. She was his prize. Max felt like an utter fool for leaving her behind to descend the stack. He never should have left her alone.

The date was June 21, 1979. Two days remained until midsummer, until the stack dropped. Two days to find Penny, exhume her, and run. Desmond said descending the stack was suicide, and after what Max had seen, he believed him. So he decided to dig instead.

He dug in the yard until his back ached, until sores opened on his hands even through the protection of his gloves. He dug until he was in danger of getting stuck in the hole, and dug a ramp out to drink water, and he went back in to dig some more. By midnight he had a hole eight feet deep by five feet wide, and he stopped to do the math. He had seen the top four levels, and it was likely there were several more below those. The bottom would be no less than forty feet deep, but probably more like seventy or eighty. And that was a pretty big assumption. It could be a hundred, for all he knew.

He'd never make it.

Would Gleaner let him leave the property long enough to rent a backhoe? It seemed unlikely. He couldn't hire anyone to come help dig, either. He would suffer no more workmen's blood on his hands, no thank you.

The stack was the only way. The most direct line to Hell. He would have to descend again, straight into the monster's lair, despite the danger. What else could he do? Penny might have gone down this way, through the dirt, but he could not follow.

Grunting with frustration at his own aging body, he speared the shovel at the bottom of the pit and heard a tiny "*tink*." It had struck something metallic.

He scooped at the earth with his hands until something gold tumbled from the mud, into his gloves. It was the odd bracelet Gleaner had given Penny. It had probably been torn from her wrist as he plunged with her below the earth, pulling her behind through the mud. She must have dug it out of the trash can, on the night after he had thrown it away. Another foolish oversight on Max's part. The ongoing stress of the siege had dulled his wits, but that was no excuse. Not when Penny's life was at stake. He had to do better from now on, no excuses. And he needed a more realistic plan.

Max sat hunched, a sad middle-aged man, in his uncomfortable modern chair. He wanted to begin immediately, to charge to Penny's rescue and be her knight in shining armor—but his old body had other plans. After stepping through the front door into the house his left knee had given out, sending him tumbling to the floor. The damage to his right shoulder had progressed beyond pain into weakness, so numb he could barely chuck the shovel into the corner of the living room. Every muscle was torn from the labor of digging; his calves, his ass, and his back screamed in pain with every step he took. Descending the stack now, without rest, really would be suicide.

So he sat, staring at the walls as the living room slowly dimmed in the twilight. In his hand he gripped Gleaner's bracelet, rubbing the rough hand-etched patterns under the carpenter's callus on his thumb. Max didn't believe in magic. He was a man of wood and tools, a staunch modern atheist; a rational guy. But as he stroked the bracelet without looking down at it, dazed in his exhaustion, he felt it vibrate in his hand. Despite his beliefs, the thing was undeniably alive.

In the quiet house, his mind kept trying to return to horrible, imaginary scenarios about what Penny might be enduring as Max rested on his overweight ass. Was she simply buried alive, shrieking in terror? Or did Gleaner have some kind of den deep below, a cave where he collected all his favorite humans? A torture chamber, perhaps, or…

Max slapped his cheek, disrupting the unhelpful chain of thought. Even that small gesture made his muscles feel like they were tearing apart. He would have to lay down.

On his bachelor-sized bed, he counted the dots on the ceiling as his brain screamed at him. What are you doing? Charge to her rescue! To hell with your tired old body. You're going down, not up! How hard could that be? You may never make it back up here anyway. Anyone can fall, though. It's the fastest way down.

He closed his eyes, willing every muscle in his body to relax, to heal. His thumb explored the tiny statue decorations on the bracelet, caressing the back of the elk-man mounted on the woman with empty eyes. The woman reminded him of Emily. Of their night in the woods, under the pines, their last and best night together.

"Max."

Emily was whispering. She touched his ear, his neck. Chills broke his skin out in goosebumps.

"Max, I'm here."

"Emily…" Max spoke in his dream, but he remained aware that he was in his room, resting on his bed. He felt Emily's presence, and a wave of guilt. "You died. I am so sorry. We tried to tell you."

"I know. I should have listened. But that's not why I'm here."

"Then why…"

"Penny. She is in pain."

Max's chest hurt. "What is he doing to her?"

"You have time to save her, but you'll have to hurry. Because he…" Emily's voice faded away.

"What? What about him? Emily!"

"…swallow her whole…"

An hour later, Max bolted upright. His spine complained at the sudden movement, but with less insistence than it had earlier. He swallowed four aspirin and touched his toes for twenty seconds, feeling the muscles loosen and stretch. No weakness remained, only pain. Good enough.

This time, he packed less. The flashlight, extra batteries, and kitchen knife fit into the loops on his tool belt, and that kept his hands free. He had to move quickly, quietly, and without any plans to return to the house when he was done. Descent was suicide. But all that mattered now was Penny.

He cast a final glance around the living room, understanding that he would never see it again. Easy come, easy go. No such thing as a free lunch. Oh well.

The sofa was still in the center of the room, where he had moved it before his previous descent. The legs had

gouged deep scratches into the wooden floor with the
repeated, forceful movement. Ha, ha. Look what I did to
your nice house. Take that, Gleaner.

After climbing down the first ladder, he turned to find
Desmond standing close, nodding his head with approval.
"You're going after her, aren't you?"

"Yeah. Any last words for me, Desmond?"

The burned man smiled in the dim, slanting light.
"Yea, though I walk through the valley of the shadow of
death…"

"Shut up."

"I shall fear no evil. For thou art with me…"

"I said shut up. That's just super unhelpful, man." Max
opened the next hatch, bracing himself for the gust of rot
and spores that would waft up from the next level.

"…comfort me." Desmond swayed, forgetting the rest
of his verse.

Max descended, gripping the sides of the hole with his
forearms, trying to preserve the strength of his leg muscles
for more difficult levels.

"Wait," Desmond whispered.

"What?"

"Kill him, Max. Kill him, kill him, kill the mad old
god."

Max swallowed. "Yeah, Desmond. I'll do my best."

The couple on the next level down greeted him with
courteous nods, and gestured toward the center of their
living room. They had rolled Mickey out for the occasion,
positioning his refrigerator in the center of the room.

"Wave at Max, Mickey," the mother crooned. "He's
going bye-bye now, to find his daughter. His lovely Penny."

The tight-packed corpse had been shaken loose from
its fungal pocket in the refrigerator; gaps had formed on
either side of the torso, where the mold had peeled away

from the plastic walls. It said nothing, but Max knew it listened. He nodded at the boy.

"Sorry he's not more talkative. He's just shy," the father said.

Max threw open the next hatch, and the found party host's top hat bobbing immediately under the opening.

"We've been expecting you," the host said, grinning up from the ladder. "Knew you couldn't keep away. Have you met Madame Ivy? She has a cousin you should meet. A lovely girl. A little plain, perhaps, but…"

"Move over. I'm coming down."

"Certainly," the host said, stepping aside.

As before, partygoers tugged at his clothing, clutched his ankles, moaned in his ear. But the room was brighter, this time. The effect was duller. Fewer moving corpses greeted his entrance; it seemed the party was dying out.

The host stepped close and stroked the front of Max's denim pants with his bony fingers. "It's so lovely to see you again."

"Fuck off."

Max pushed the guests aside and charged toward the hall, heading for the bedroom with the hatch while simultaneously trying to think of a plan to handle the beast he knew waited below. The mastiff had been locked in a house-shaped cage filled with its own shed hair for decades. Maybe it was starved for attention. What did dogs like? Petting was not an option. Tennis balls? There were none of those here. Bones…

Bones.

Max spun around back toward the living room, and reached the host in three long strides. Before the host could protest, Max seized his right arm—the one which had grabbed and stroked him without his permission.

Well, that certainly wouldn't happen again.

"In heaven's name, what are you…" the host started, before catching on to what Max was doing. "Don't you dare! I'll have you know I'm a very famous…"

Max was grabbed from behind by a thin man in an elf's hat and a glamorously painted female corpse in a blue ball gown, but the attack had no strength. He shoved them back, and they tumbled to the floor on either side like dolls. As Max ripped the host's arm from his body, the corpse screeched, a high and affronted sound. Every party guest dropped their drink and screeched along with their mentor in sympathy and rage. They rushed at Max, slapping at him with weak, bony arms. Kicking and thrashing, he tore free of the group to run back down the hall to the hatch, gripping the host's arm in his hand.

The master bedroom was staler than last time, drier. The smears of blood had faded from red to brown, and the hanging severed limbs which had been plump had turned to bone covered in skin like crepe paper. The mayhem was winding down, hushed in anticipation of the collapse of the stack.

Max opened the hatch, wielding the flashlight in his right hand and the host's severed arm in his left. With the thick odor of old dog hair overwhelming his senses, he jumped down.

CHAPTER 22 – The Wapiti of 1939

The day John's son was born was the best day of his life.

The boy came out looking just like him, the very spirit 'n image. Same elongated nose, crooked smile, round ears. Even had a little mole on his left cheek, just a bit lower than his da's was.

Colin was a miracle boy. Annie was barren, the doctors had all agreed. They sat behind their desks wearing their big bottle-bottom glasses, nodding and frowning about what a horribly sterile womb poor old Annie had. Lifeless as a desert—or, perhaps, as a morgue, considering how many babies she had already lost.

The couple's marriage was a sad one, up until little Colin was born. He was a strong lad, stronger than all the odds which had been stacked against him.

Annie glowed, barren no longer, a fount of youth and of Mother Nature's own holy grace. She gripped that baby to her chest, fed it from her breast, and worshipped him like he was a tiny god.

Colin was especially active whenever John held him. The boy looked around at the world with his big eyes, reached for his father's nose, smiled, kicked, laughed. But he calmed in his mother's embrace, still and peaceful, surrendering all his trust to her protective arms. The boy was night and day between mother and father, and always, always wonderful.

When he was only ten months old, he took his first steps. Stumbling like a drunken sailor, he let go of the sofa, shuffled across the rug, and only fell down when his foot caught in the handle of the old basement hatch that was set into the floor. He bumped his head on the boards and cried, but only for a minute. He was a good boy, and it would take more than that to keep him down.

His favorite food was peas. His favorite color was orange. He liked listening to the Amos 'n' Andy radio show, and watching the birds flit among the pines through the window. When John returned home every day from his work as a foreman at the logging camp, Annie handed the boy to him as soon as he walked through the door. And when she was done cooking dinner, he handed the boy back. They were the happiest family in the world, John reckoned. How could any on earth be happier?

And so the depth of their grief was even greater than their happiness had ever been when the boy died in the winter of 1937. It was a cursed year. Amelia Earhart had disappeared, the Hindenburg had blown up, and police were killing innocents in the streets of Chicago. In that year of loss and death, was it any wonder the miracle child also succumbed to God's wrath?

He went as peaceful as he had arrived, asleep in his crib. Heaven had sent them an angel, but it was only on loan, and when the term was up he had been repossessed by the Lord, whose will could not be known.

Dark times descended upon the couple as they did upon the world. Annie flew into a storm of rage that never ceased. She snarled like a beast, and tore at John's skin with her nails when he tried to embrace her. Night after night, she lashed out at him, at the house, at God in his heavenly throne. Spouting evil words in the devil's tongue, she swore vengeance upon the Lord himself, and promised her soul to Satan in exchange for the return of her boy. John brought priests and doctors in endless procession, but none could lead the woman out from the depths of her madness.

Colin was just another crib death. A common enough

way for a child to die, if a sad one. But there was nothing common about it for Annie. Colin was her last chance, the doctors had said. Her womb had suffered too much trauma over the years to ever bear another.

John resorted to tying her down at night so she could not harm herself as he slept. All sharp objects were removed from the house. He stayed home from the sawmill for months on end to protect her from her ravings, but it was not a permanent fix. He needed to return to work, or they would both starve.

Finally, John spotted an ad in the local Downieville newspaper that turned a light on in his mind. It was a crazy idea, but worth a try: MASTIFF PUPS. GOOD PRICE. 472 PINE RIDGE. ASK FOR CHARLIE.

Against John's protestations, Annie named the puppy "Colin." The naming seemed unhealthy, even unnatural. But Annie would have it no other way.

The puppy grew up much as its predecessor had; an easy babe to raise, rarely crying, playful with John and serene with Annie. She doted on it as she had on her son, curling up with him in front of the fireplace on cold nights, cooking his meals from scratch, teaching him and cooing to him as she cradled him in her arms. Her devotion to her son transferred to the dog in its entirety.

John nearly regretted buying the pup, but Annie had stopped threatening her own health, at least. Something in her brain had snapped with the death of her son, and if the dog brought her some peace, then so be it.

As Annie calmed, John was able to return to work. When he arrived home every day, Annie passed the puppy into his arms as she had their son, and John dutifully stroked the pup's head and smiled before setting it down to take his jacket off.

By the time the dog was a year old, it had become horrendously spoiled. It barked whenever it pleased, chewed the legs off the furniture, and still believed it belonged in John's lap although it weighed nearly 200 pounds. The household belonged to Colin, as the couple catered to its every whim; Annie because of her emotional transference to the dog, and John because he wanted to preserve his wife's sanity. But the animal tore their relationship apart as surely as it did their furniture.

Annie would neither surrender the dog nor chastise it when it misbehaved. When John tried to correct its behavior, she would cry, and her suicidal tendencies would return. And so he was no longer head of his own household, or even a close second. Yet he worked hard to keep Annie and Colin housed and fed, a slave to the beast and its mistress.

At two years old, the mastiff became more aggressive. Its temperament changed as it reached its full weight of 350 pounds. It snarled to make its demands known, and did whatever it pleased. For it knew John was no match; Colin was, undeniably, the alpha. Whenever John raised his voice or even made a sudden movement, the dog's head would whip around and its lip would twitch, and John would tremble in fear.

The end came during an autumn storm in 1938. The heavens opened up and cried, pouring rain on Downieville in amounts greater than any in recorded history. Wind knocked out the radio tower. The clouds crashed and cracked with a constant roaring that set the mastiff on edge. It lay on the floor, shaking with fear at the sound.

John sat frozen in his chair, afraid to move. The dog would blame him for the storm, no doubt. And then what would happen? Annie cooked extra food for Colin that night, all his favorites; a whole chicken, a side of beef, a bowl of salted greens. John sat in the corner of the living room sipping from a bowl of oatmeal, watching the dog refuse plate after plate of hot home-cooked food.

Annie sobbed, sure the beast would die of hunger that very night. John sneered. The monster was well fed, and one night without food could never affect the creature's health. No, if anything, it would be stronger than ever, unburdened by the weight of its evening meal.

As John spoke those truths to Annie, a bolt of lightning shot down from the sky to strike a tree at the side of the house. If the house had not been flat-roofed, it might have struck the building and dissipated. But instead it struck a tree, and the tree was lit ablaze with an explosion of electrical fire.

Colin panicked. He leapt to his feet, raised his hackles in a wide stripe down his back, and barked in a strange voice John had never heard before. It was the cry of a dog who was enraged and frightened all at once, gone mad with fury and fear.

Snarling, Colin leapt. John's oatmeal tumbled to the floor from his open hand as the dog tore out his throat and shook his body back and forth like a doll. Annie screamed when Colin dropped John and turned to her with his face coated in her husband's blood, and only then did her mind clear. She saw the dog for what it was; a truly evil beast, and one of her own making.

Colin snapped her neck in his jaw, paralyzing her. She could not feel his teeth as they dug into her stomach to tear out her barren womb, but she could hear everything. The ripping, the growling, the slipping of the dog's feet in the flow of blood which pooled out under her body. She wanted to cry; her womb had been useless, but it was hers, and Colin had no right to it.

No, Colin was not his name. The beast was only a dog.

Colin had been…Who? Her baby boy.

Finally, her memory of her son came back in a rush. How had she forgotten her own poor child? She had shielded the painful memory of his death from the rest of her mind in a desperate act to save her sanity, but that had been a mistake. Annie's final thoughts as the creature emptied her stomach of its organs was of her son's smile, the special one he only offered to her as he fell to sleep in her arms.

The dog lived on for several more months, sustained first by the flesh of its owners, and later by what it could hunt in the forest. It claimed the house as its own den, and even the wild animals learned not to wander onto the lot. It roamed through the pines as would a lion, howling its madness to any who could hear. But the native animals of the woods knew the dog's end was near, and they waited.

When the stack dropped in 1939, the dog went with it, and the forest was peaceful once more.

CHAPTER 23

Max didn't really want to hurt the dog.

As a child, he had raised and loved a St. Bernard; a 140-pound cuddle-bug named Muffy. When she was a puppy, she resembled a teddy bear with a white stripe up her nose. By the time she was six months old, she could lick Max's face from his chin to his forehead in a single long swipe of her tongue. He had been forced to leave her behind when he went away to college, and she died soon after that. His mother said she had died of old age, but Max had always worried in his heart that the dog had mourned his abandonment of her, and passed away from loneliness. That guilt returned to him now.

He had no stomach to harm this mastiff, but he also understood that nothing in the stack was sane, and he might be stuck between two bad choices. His best bet was to find the hatch as quickly as possible, and descend without alerting the dog.

There was no sign of the animal when he landed on the soft piles of bug-ridden fur. He began shuffling his feet without delay, first the right, then the left, hoping his toe would snag on a door handle. His foot struck an object, but it moved easily across the floor, clattering across the boards; that couldn't be it. His other toe caught on the edge of a rug, then collided with an object which felt like a plate or a bowl. Lying hidden below the ocean of hair was the shattered debris of the family which used to live here. Who were they? And why did only their dog endure the dropping of the stack?

Something shifted at the end of the hall. There was movement in the master bedroom. It had to be the dog.

Max tightened his grip on the skeletal arm he had torn from the party host upstairs. Hopefully, the dog would stay put. Barring that, perhaps it would like the treat he brought. The kitchen knife tucked in his tool belt was a last resort.

Max hastened toward the kitchen, scooping rolling piles of hair ahead of his shins. It swept back in oily mats, revealing the floor underneath. Great splotches of dry blood stained the linoleum near the bony remains of the previous residents. Either they had died in the kitchen, or had been dragged here by the dog some time later. It must have recognized the kitchen as a place to eat, which might mean it had been domesticated at some point in the past. Maybe, one day long ago, it had been a good boy.

The sound of heavy breathing moved down the hallway. The dog had smelled him, even over the thick reek of decaying hair. Max could duck under the fluff, scoop it over his body, and try to hide—but his stomach recoiled at the thought. There was only so much a man could take.

He backtracked, and peeked around the corner into the living room. The dog was stalking past the entryway, flaring its nostrils, heading for the kitchen's other entrance. If he got far enough, Max could give him the run-around.

As soon as the dog's shoulders disappeared from view, Max sprinted for the hallway. He leapt over a low mound which was probably supported underneath by an ancient sofa, hit his shin on an end-table-shaped heap, and barrelled down the hall toward the middle bedroom, the one which mirrored his workshop. As he reached out his hand for the doorknob, his foot finally found what it had been searching for all along.

His left big toe caught neatly under the hatch handle and sent him sprawling into the wall, colliding with enough force to leave a man-sized crater in the plaster.

From the kitchen came an alarmed bark. Max's presence had definitely been noticed now. He would have only seconds to pry open the hatch and escape. But when he turned back toward the handle, he frowned with dismay. The hair had rolled back over the hatch, and he would have to dig for the handle again.

Falling to his hands and knees, he swept back and forth for the hatch. The dog had spotted him, and was nearing; it raised its lips in a snarl, displaying rows of yellowed teeth.

"Good boy," Max whispered. "Stay."

The dog barked again, enraged. It was, apparently, not a good boy after all. It lunged at Max just as his fingers found the hatch handle, and with his other hand he raised the severed arm he had brought as tribute. Either the sudden movement or the gift distracted the dog, and it stopped in its tracks, confused. Max tossed the arm into the kitchen, and as the dog stood trying to decide which prey to devour first, Max flung open the hatch and leapt into the darkness below.

Max had been prepared for almost anything this time. What would it be? A torture chamber in the shape of a modestly appointed sitting room? Perhaps a zombie family, all sitting down for their daily meal of rotting brains. The stack had proved anything was possible, so long as it was awful.

What he had not expected was water. He torpedoed several feet deep into a small lake with his lips pressed shut, trying not to take any of the liquid in. He kicked until he found air, but it was dank and choking. The water had a slick, oily feel to it, and the surface layer supported a slimy gel laced with algae and wispy, leggy pond-striders. The bugs were pure white, turned albino by endless generations of living in total darkness.

Max paddled, trying to stay afloat, but the weight of his clothing and tool belt threatened to drag him under. He abandoned his shoes, but in his struggle to detach the tool belt he swallowed a mouthful of the foul pond and immediately retched it back up, adding to the disgusting soup.

Kicking and cursing, he found a wall to cling to. He was in the hallway near the master bedroom doorway, but his flashlight, submersed in the water, was flickering on and off. If he didn't find his way out soon, he would lose his only source of light.

The water filled the house up to within a foot from the ceiling. The air was thin, and sour with mildew. Max kept his free hand pressed against the wall, directing his light down at the floor under the water. Somewhere down there was a hatch.

His flashlight found not a hatch, but a round ball floating in the water. Max groaned, understanding; it was a head. Of course there were dead bodies here.

Of course.

He intentionally blurred his vision, squinting to block out the details of the corpse floating past his feet. It caught a current, and made its way down the hallway on a mission of its own. A minute later, Max found another body, this one snagged on a living room lamp. It was small, dwarfish—but no, it was only a half. The pelvis and legs drifted near the sofa, and the head bobbed atop the water like a pool toy. Max batted it away and continued his grim search, wading toward the kitchen.

The water there was murkier, contaminated by old food and two more bodies as well as flora which had grown from their nutrients. Green moss reached up like a network of spidery trees, tangling around Max's ankles, brushing his bare feet with tender strokes. The floor was obscured by plant life, but he thought he could see a small irregularity, something set into the floor that resembled a hinge. He would have to dive to be sure.

Another problem had Max worried, almost as much as the sickening pool. His heart was throbbing in his chest, pounding on his sternum like a door knocker. Perhaps it was only fear, perhaps not. He should have jogged more, ate more salad in his 30s. Too many cigarettes, and too many six-bourbon days. But was it all his fault, really? Who could have anticipated any of this?

"All right, Max," he said into the darkness. "You listen to me now. You're going to dive for that hatch, and you're not going to die while you're doing it. Got it?"

No one answered.

"Good." He took a deep breath, deep enough to hurt his ribs, and kicked his feet up toward the ceiling. The weeds that entangled his ankles wrapped around themselves in knots, restricting his swimming. He had to stop, reach back, and rip the strands away from his legs, wasting precious breath. Bubbles rushed out from his nose. He would have to resurface and start again.

Just as he poked his head above the water, something struck the surface in another room. The impact created waves throughout the house, pushing flotsam out in all directions. Twitching pond-striders rode on in mats of moss which Max batted away before they could shipwreck in his hair. Whatever had landed in the water was thrashing and churning to stay afloat. An angry bark confirmed what Max had feared. The dog had worked up enough courage and anger to follow him down through the hatch.

He would have to work faster. Inhaling and exhaling until his lungs felt stretched out, he sucked in as much stale air as he could hold and made a final push for what he hoped was the hatch. Streamers of moss and human hair caught on his fingers, but he pressed forward until he found the edge of the little door and pried at it with his nails. It was reluctant to open, swollen by decades spent underwater, and as he scratched at it in desperation his lungs began to cry for oxygen. The dog paddled into the kitchen behind him, creating extra waves, moving Max beyond his reach of the door. Out of control, he bumped into the kitchen wall, and returned again to the surface for air.

He found himself nearly nose-to-nose with the mastiff. For the first time, he could truly appreciate the size of the beast. The dog could take Max's entire head in its mouth if it wished, and it seemed determined to do so. It had abandoned the treat Max had brought for him, deciding he was the bigger prize.

"Bad dog! No! Get outta here!" Max shouted, but his words seemed to encourage it. Barking over and over, the dog kicked in the water, bounding closer to Max and forcing him to plunge back underwater, kicking toward the hatch.

"Last chance," he thought. "This is it. Get your shit together, or die. And if you die, so does Penny."

This time, he used all of his strength to pry the hatch open, grimacing and letting the rest of his air bubble away as he did. A fingernail was split in half and his thumbs were bruised, but the hatch finally separated from its frame.

Water drained from the kitchen in a massive rush, drawing every item in the house toward the hole. The opening would not last; it would clog soon, stuffed with moss and hair and old kitchenware. Max dived for it while it lasted, throwing himself toward the opening, ignoring all else to pull his body through the hole.

As he landed on the next level, the floor crumbled

under the weight of his falling body combined with the gushing water. Then he fell through another, and another; he struck powdered drywall, splintered wood, rotting fabric, first disintegrating in dry puffs of dust before mixing with the water to create a waterfall of dark, sticky sludge as Max smashed down through level after ancient level until he entered a vast underground cavern.

He fell further, suspended in silence for several seconds as the ceiling pulled away above. The last story was no ten-foot-tall kitchen or outdated living room, but instead a stony cave, massive and hollow and quiet except for the roar of pouring water from the upper levels. He landed on his side on a surface that broke his fall but snapped beneath his body. A gush of stagnant water arrived with him, trickling to a halt after he landed. Far above, where the hatch was, something had clogged the hole; Max could see the dark pelt of the mastiff crushed into the opening, its body acting as a stopper. It squirmed for a moment, then howled a low, mournful howl, then went still.

CHAPTER 24

The room Max had fallen into was not like the other levels of the stack. The intermittent flicker of his dying flashlight showed him that the chunk of collapsed ceiling which had arrived with him had landed among a scattered assortment of stone benches, hewn in place from the rocky ground by archaic hammers and chisels. There was no method to their arrangement; the seats faced in every direction, permanently fixed in their chaotic placement.

Some of the benches more or less faced massive wall decorations that resembled altars. Shelves covered in wax candles and dried flowers were mounted under the preserved heads of a variety of woodland creatures. The largest altar, at the end of the room, featured not an animal but a human skull. Powdery stacks of bones were placed beneath the altar as ritual offerings, arranged in geometric shapes.

At the far end of the room a soft voice said, "Hello."

Max shouted in surprise, backed up, and tripped over one of the stone benches. Narrowly avoiding hitting his head on the next bench, he cradled the flashlight to his chest to break its fall.

The voice giggled. "Sorry if I startled you."

"Who are you?"

"Get up first, then we'll talk."

Max's body wanted to stay. He was so tired, even laying down by accident triggered an overwhelming desire to sleep. But he forced his body up, hoisting himself atop a stone bench before getting his wobbly legs under his weight.

"Well, that's better," the voice said.

Max shined his flashlight in the direction of the speaker, and found a woman standing at the entrance to the room. Her robes were embroidered with ornate patterns of birds and flowers and stars which reminded Max of Penny's treehouse paintings. On her head was pressed a crown of dry flowers and leaves. A tight strip of cloth was tied over her eyes, blocking her vision. And her face…

"Oh my god…Emily? You can't be…"

The woman smiled. "No. I am not her. Wouldn't that have been nice, though? Tell me."

"Tell you what?"

"Tell me how nice it would have been."

Max frowned. "Well, it would have meant she wasn't dead."

"And that would be…?"

"Well, it would be nice. I didn't hate her." Max shook his head. "We weren't on the best terms, but I didn't want her to die. Not that it's any of your business, whoever you are."

"You were attracted to her, weren't you?"

The woman stepped closer to the light, and Max could see that she did not resemble Emily as much as he first thought; the hair was a different color, the skin tone lighter. But she could have been her cousin, or sister.

"You don't need to know my name," the woman said. "But perhaps you would welcome my guidance."

"What is this place?"

"It is a temple, and it is older than you can imagine. It was built to worship a god of enormous power in the time before men kept written records of their thoughts and works."

"Gleaner. It was built for him, wasn't it?"

"I don't know that name. But the god who these people revered could change his form. Sometimes he appeared as an elk, or a man with great horns, or a…"

"A hare."

The woman smiled. Her lips parted, revealing elongated canine teeth. "Certainly. Do you know him?"

"Gleaner? I've met him."

"Well, what did you think?" The woman sat on a stone bench and crossed her legs. She had navigated the room without hesitation despite her blindness, as though she had lived there for a thousand years.

"He's a monster, a murderer. Not someone worth worshiping."

"But he's also wonderfully powerful. Don't you agree? And when something is much, much more powerful than you are, maybe that does, in fact, make it worth worshiping. Maybe that is what makes it beautiful."

"No. He isn't beautiful. He's just evil."

The woman grinned, displaying a row of fine, pointed teeth. "Ah, evil! And what is more powerful than evil? Nothing, I think. Worship should be at least considered, in that case."

"I don't have time for this. I'm sorry, but I have to go. He has my daughter, Penny…somewhere down here, and I need to find her. Have you seen…" Max caught himself. She could not have seen anything. She was blind. "Have you heard any strange noises? Like, a girl screaming?"

"Hmm. I heard the scuttle of rats, just over there," the woman said, gesturing to a corner of the room with a languid motion of her hand. "And over that way, the earthworms are particularly noisy today."

"What does that have to do with Penny?"

"With whom?"

"I don't have time for this Wonderland bullshit. I'm going." He wiped the remaining drops of water from his flashlight, cast a quick, hopeless glance around the room for his abandoned boots, and straightened his sore back. "Goodbye. And thanks, uh, I guess."

The woman stood, and looped her arm around his. "Help me get to my home first, will you? It's just over there."

Max shook her loose. "No, I'm sorry. I just don't have time. I have to go now."

The ground outside the temple consisted of loose plates of shifting shale, a treacherous kind of terrain for shoeless feet. Max stepped carefully, but as each flat chunk slid under his weight, several more noisily clattered down the path which sloped away from the temple door. When he stepped wrong, the edges of the rocks cut into his skin. He couldn't go on like this; there had to be another way.

He stopped in place to consider his options, but the ground continued to move, carrying him down along with it. When he reached the bottom of the hill, the shale ended at a ruined street paved with broken cobblestones and sandy grout. Rows of ramshackle hovels lined each side of the street, with miniature versions of the temple altars installed over every doorway. Each had the skull of a deer, or a dog, or a rabbit, with dried flowers stuffed in the eye sockets and stains running down its jaw.

"Ah, the homes of the devoted," the woman said behind him. She had followed in perfect silence, with her hands clasped in front of her dress in an attitude of reverence. "Those poor souls did not survive the initial collapse. But their faith had been faltering, even before. Perhaps that was the true reason for their fate."

"The collapse?"

"Of the stack. They were the first, and the city you walk through now holds the crumbled remains of many, many more. It is a depository of wonderful dreams, it is," she whispered. "It surely is."

"If you say so," Max muttered, picking his way through the cobbles. "So—and correct me if I'm wrong— you're some kind of ghost? I assume you used to live here."

The woman giggled. "I still do, obviously. Why, I've always lived here."

"Okay. Then either tell me how to find Gleaner, or leave me alone."

"So impertinent," the woman said, frowning. It was the first disapproving expression she had made since Max arrived, and he found it as unsettling as her smile.

"Sorry. But like I said, my daughter..."

"Oh, fine then. You're no fun. Go straight here, then turn left at the end of the street."

As Max passed the homes, he peeked inside. The interiors reminded him of pictures he had seen of Pompeii. Food sat in bowls on tables coated in thousands of years of dust. Bones littered the ground, both animal and human. The rocky ceiling overhead was impenetrable, so the remains of the town had been preserved in darkness since the day of its destruction.

"What happened to this place?"

"Something awful. They must have angered a god. A very, very powerful old god."

"What do you mean, 'must have'? Don't you know? I thought you'd always lived here."

The woman's cold smile returned, but she said nothing.

At the end of the street, Max turned left. Another long avenue stretched out before him, lined with larger buildings. Some were two stories tall, with windows that overlooked the walkways. The shattered remnants of carts and furniture littered the street, and something had left deep gouges on many of the walls. Most buildings had deep score-marks in sets of four, as though a massive animal had clawed them in rage.

"What did that?" Max pointed at the scrapes.

"Something powerful. Something large. Someone handsome."

"What?"

"Power is beauty, is it not? So whatever it was, must have been very handsome."

"You're crazy."

The woman laughed. Each of her teeth came to a fine point, as if filed—and they looked bigger than they had a few minutes ago.

"I'm not crazy," the woman said. "That's not my name. But you can call me Puck."

"*You!*" Max's hands made fists. "You are the one who threatened me and Penny! But on the phone you sounded like a man."

"That's a horribly closed-minded view, Max. I also have been called Loki, and Pan, and sometimes Gleaner… although that name is not my favorite, and I don't answer to it. But all of those names are wrong, of course. I am none of those people."

"Then who are you? What are you really?"

"I am beyond your comprehension." The woman transformed into a man with antlers, and continued to grow into an elk, and finally shrunk to the hare which had watched from the woods. The only aspect which remained unchanged in each transformation were the eyes, red-ringed with black diamond pupils. "I am the last of many, the final remnant of a pantheon of gods, and I am in my end years. But I am very, very beautiful. Don't you agree?"

The creature morphed into a goat, a flock of birds, a pile of throbbing flesh. It settled, finally, on the form of a St. Bernard, like the pet dog Max had owned as a child. But it was far too large to be a dog; fourteen feet tall from head to floor, with teeth the length of Max's flashlight.

"Stay away from me," Max whispered. "And tell me where to find Penny." His flashlight flickered again; it was in its last minutes of life.

The St Bernard laughed as it moved closer, breathing on Max with heavy gusts of foul air. "How arrogant of you to make demands! Obviously, you can't make me do anything. I am Legion. I am All."

Max drew his fist back and punched. The slick slime on the massive dog's nose deflected his weak hand, but he still wore Gleaner's gold bracelet. When the metal scraped against the skin, the creature threw its head back, screaming as it transformed against its will into a smaller figure—that of the elk man, naked, hunched over the inanimate form of a faceless woman with empty-hole eyes. His form matched the sculpture on the bracelet.

The creature screeched in frustration and tore itself up from the ground, dismounting its mate. Hooves sprouted from its hands and its back legs lengthened, but Max touched it again with the bracelet, and the new growths receded, once again forcing the elk-man to bow low over his immobile bride.

"You…can't…" Gleaner huffed.

"Apparently I can," Max said, wielding the bracelet over the back of his hand like brass knuckles. "Now, tell me how to find Penny or I'll never let you out of this form again."

The elk-man rose, standing before Max, grandly nude. Max diverted his eyes.

"What are you afraid of, Max?" Gleaner said, grinning. "Look at me. Gaze upon my godly beauty. Desire me."

"You're crazy."

"Yes. About that, at least, you were warned."

The elk-man formed rear hooves and stamped the ground until the cobblestones crumbled. He jumped, bounded, smashed his hooves into the floor until it collapsed, taking Gleaner with it before Max could get near enough to touch him again with the bracelet. The elk-man plunged into the darkness below, laughing as he fell.

There was still one more level to go, it seemed. And it was one of pure liquid night, with no floor that Max's flashlight could find.

CHAPTER 25

Max cursed himself for a coward. He called himself names. Chickenshit, wimp, weakling, craven gutless jellyfish. But his insults had no effect. He couldn't make himself jump in the hole.

It was bottomless, endless, darker than dark. Anything at all could be down there—or worse, nothing. Just empty space, through which Max would forever plummet into an infinite void, screaming until his voice gave out, crying and pissing his pants for endless days until panic or dehydration finally granted him the release of death. And even then, it wouldn't end, would it? His lifeless body would persist along its downward journey, tumbling in silence, a corpse bomb that would explode if it eventually met with either a floor or perhaps the center of the earth. It was a fate worse than being buried alive, for it would take days for him to die, falling alone and terrified in a continuous everlasting night.

It seemed impossible that Penny was alive, somewhere down there. How much time did he have left? It seemed like he had been crawling down the stack a week, but it could not have been more than hours. The passage of time in the depths was uncountable, and his persistent anxiety further blurred the measure of days.

The pit at his feet instilled in him a combination of a fear of heights, considering the relative height of his own position, and a sense of dread which accompanied his increasing consciousness of the layers and stories above his head. The heaviness of the earth above weighed upon him with a growing awareness of how unlikely it was that he would ever see the sky again. Here, in this abandoned city

from before time began, there was no life; no tree roots
penetrated so deep, no scrubby grass grew between the
cobbles or moss on the walls. The cavern was an arcane
cauldron, and Max a shivering morsel of meat in a sterile
bowl where no living plant or creature could survive.
The drain at the top still dripped stagnant water from the
upper levels, and the drain at the bottom threatened to
swallow Max whole if he could only work up the courage
to…

Jump.

His feet tingled, but did not move. He thought of
Penny, smiling as she took a bite of a homemade cookie,
dutifully organizing her homework, training her cat with
love even when the creature hissed and scratched at her
arm. Max could not abandon her. She was his greatest
accomplishment, the source of all his pride. So…

Jump.

His right toe nudged forward. A beginning, but not
enough.

He couldn't go back up, anyway. The opening to the
bottom of the real stack—the one made of living rooms
and bedrooms and kitchens—was thirty feet over the
ground. It would take days, and more strength than he
possessed, to create a mound of debris high enough to
reach the hole. And he would be carrying with him the
additional burden of guilt at abandoning his daughter to
the whims of the mad old god. No, going back was not an
option. He had two choices; die here, alone in this city of
ancient grief, or…

Jump.

Max's knees buckled in terror at the sudden knowledge that his brain had already made the final decision.
He did not leap into the hole so much as stumble, half of
his body still yearning to find a grip on the edge before he

went through while the rest of his energy pushed him forward and down, down into the gaping mouth that led to nowhere. He turned as he fell, watching the dim opening to the cavern shrink and fade away as it receded. The sensation was strong that he was not falling, but that the rest of the world was fleeing him, leaving him in utter solitude.

For several seconds, he was resigned to the knowledge that his pessimism had been correct. This pit had no bottom. He would die, spinning in the air, feeling his body dry out in the relentless winds of gravity—but there, below him, was a light.

His dread of never finding the pit's floor was overlapped by a sudden terror of landing, and he kicked in the air, panicking as the details of the approaching level became more visible. In every direction, from the spot directly below and on to the horizon on each side, lay a vast labyrinth. The walls were built inconsistently; some were leafy green, some were brown, others shining black like obsidian. It was not a simple puzzle maze, but rather it was populated by beastly creatures and creeping plants. And directly below, the largest tree Max had ever seen was blocking his descent.

He crashed into it, catching a thick branch under his armpit as a prickly bunch of twigs tore under the back of his shirt, leaving a patchwork of bloody scratches. His lower back smacked into another large branch before he caught a thinner bough in his hand, using it to slow his fall. A thick wooden prong embedded itself in the side of his foot and snapped off, digging deeper every time it struck another obstacle. He landed on his side near the base of the trunk, at the core of a messy ball of leaves and debris, covered in lacerations. But he was alive.

Max's arrival did not go unnoticed. Cries rose up from the labyrinth announcing the newcomer. They sounded like hunting calls. Above the din rose a muddle of sharper yelps, like those of large dogs, but maddened, depraved, and starving.

The fragment of wood protruding from his foot was shaped like a bee's stinger, four inches long with rough edges. Pulling on it made his head spin and his vision fade; it was in deep, and dirty. But it had to come out. There was no way he could walk with it lodged in place.

He needed a distraction, something like a mantra, to focus his mind. Staring at the broken pieces of his flashlight, he hummed under his breath. What were the words to that song, that one song with the really great bass line…

"Everybody's got a little light under the sun," he wheezed, pinching the spike between his thumb and first finger. "Under the sun, under the sun…" He yanked hard, but the thorn moved slow. He could feet every millimeter of its progress on its way out of his flesh. But it did go, leaving behind a mess of dirt and tiny splinters caked in blood. He tore a strip of his tattered shirt sleeve and bound both his feet, creating makeshift socks.

The tree was too tall to see its top. Its leaves were almond-shaped, clustered in thick bunches that branched off from sturdy arms spread wide from the trunk, which was thirty feet in diameter. The behemoth stood in the center of a clearing in which it did not quite fit; its branches leaned out over the walls of the labyrinth, shading the paths that ran parallel. At the corner of the tree's yard was a doorway set in the wall, and in the entryway sat a hare with red eyes and black diamond pupils. It was watching him.

"Gleaner," Max said. "No more tricks. Where is my daughter?"

"She's my daughter now," the hare said. "Possession is nine-tenths of the law, you know. And she is possessed…

by me! You wouldn't even recognize her." Gleaner giggled.

"Take me. Let her go. Let her leave the stack, and keep me instead."

"I don't want you as much as I want her. But right now I have you both. You've already lost the game, Max."

"I'll do anything."

"True," the hare said, scratching behind its ear with a foot. "And that idea has some merit. But you have no chips, Max. Nothing to barter, nothing to wager. I already have all that you are."

"There must be something."

"All you have is your life, and all I really need that you can offer is entertainment."

"What do you…"

"Be the jackal."

"What?"

"Did you know that British colonists hunted jackals when there were no foxes to be found? You are no fox, Max. You are not clever, or quick, or beautiful. You are dull, timid, and frail. So, you will be my jackal."

Max shook his head. "I don't know what you mean."

"I'll see you at the hunt, Max. And 'ware the hounds." The hare grinned, and turned tail to disappear into the hedgerow. Where it had sat, the ground was smeared with blood and fine white fur.

Max's footwraps did not last more than an hour before fraying and falling away. By the time they were gone, he hardly noticed; every corner he turned revealed a new terror, a fresh obstruction to chip away at his hope and his sanity. His left foot-wrap had disappeared as he fled from a teeming swarm of malignant rats which poured from the cracks in the labyrinth walls. The right one, which had bound his injury, sloughed away after the rains began, as

bolts of twisted lightning shot out of the cloudless sky to
slam into the pointed column tops that marked each turn
of the maze.

Stumbling and disoriented, he lost the remains of his
confidence. Lost also was his knife, and Gleaner's gold
bracelet. The tool belt he still wore, which held up his sodden pants in the downpour he was unable to shelter from.
Left, right, left, right. Max was a mouse, and Penny was
the prize, but how much longer would she be alive? Surely
the stack was due to drop, and that was his deadline, even
though the house itself had been left far behind. Gleaner's
power was peaking.

More imminently ominous was the distant cry of
the dogs. Max was being hunted, and the nearer the pack
came, the faster his time ran out. He had to find Penny
before the hunting party found him, or all hope was lost.
Gleaner had not reappeared since their conversation near
the ash tree. He was allowing his minions to terrorize
Max, wear him down. Massive black birds flew overhead,
screeching like women screaming. A human figure with
four gangly legs tracked Max, following him along the tops
of the walls, never attacking but always watching with its
circular yellow eyes. It relayed his position to something
else which never stopped following; a harlequin grotesque
in white face paint with greasy black diamonds over its
eyes, dragging an axe the size of a telephone pole. Max
easily outpaced the creature but it never, ever stopped
marching on. After only five minutes of rest, the incessant
scraping of the axehead would catch up, following in his
footsteps with plodding persistence. The white-painted
face would loom through the faded underground light,
wrenching into a wide grin as its grip tightened on its axe
handle, preparing to swing the sharpened blade at Max's
skull. So on and on he would scurry, exhausted and weep-

ing. The insectoid scout would mirror him atop the walls, the mime would follow, and the march went ever forward.

Much of the path was uprooted. He stumbled over broken cobblestones, twisting his ankle, grinding muck into his open wound. Sometimes the baying dogs would draw close and he would freeze in terror with nowhere to run, but they always pulled away before stumbling into his section of the labyrinth. It was only a matter of time before they found the correct hallway, and his rescue mission would end.

Worse than any of this was Penny's cry. Sometimes, over the howling of the dogs, Max heard her desperate sobs. The sound reassured him that she was alive, but the anguish in her voice tore at his heart. He wanted to respond, let her know he was on his way, but such a foolish action would give away his position. He could only listen from afar, try to choose his next turn wisely, and pin his hope on luck that he would find the center of Hell before Gleaner reached the apex of his strength.

For hours he stumbled. Left, right, left. A swarm of slick-black beetles with webbed membrane wings buzzed around his head, tangling in his hair. He batted them away and trudged on. His wounded foot ached for a while, then throbbed, then went numb. The maze was endless, hundreds of miles in diameter, thousands of miles of path, and time was running short.

Left, right. The path he was on cleared and became smoother. Perhaps he was on the right track; this section was less dilapidated than most of the others. He turned again, toward the direction he thought Penny's cries were the loudest, but was forced back around again, going the wrong way. Two turns later, he was on a mushy trail that seemed familiar. He looked down and saw red, bloody footprints. His own footprints. He had been here before.

Shuddering and sobbing, he leaned against the stone wall to rest. It was all for nothing; he hadn't seen this passage for two hours. Two hours lost, two hours of Penny's life slipping away. The dark creature which was trailing him perched on the wall above his head, breathing hard, darting its eyes between his position and the grinning mummer which followed. Max had only minutes before he was overtaken. His pace was slowing as his strength ebbed.

Penny sobbed. With a pounding heart, Max pressed on. Right, left. Moving away from his old bloody footprints, creating new ones. The call of the hounds echoed among the stony walls, becoming louder after each crack of lightning, excited by their master's display of power. To the right, in the distance, the maze stretched up over a low hill, and at the top was a squat tower of brick with a flat roof. And there, standing atop the tower, Gleaner gazed out over his realm. He was in a new form, one Max had never seen before; a massive bear.

Eighteen feet tall and heavy enough to crack the roof of the tower on which he stood, Gleaner observed the labyrinthine hellscape. Six eyes in two diagonal rows, arranged in his head like a spider's, glowed as bright as jack-o-lanterns. The embers burned deep within the creature's skull as his eldritch power grew and coursed through his body. Below the place where he stood there was a gate, and behind the gate was Penny.

Max's mime stalker turned the corner, and the scraping of the axe became loud. He had lost track. The dark scout cackled with gleeful anticipation from its position on the wall, watching the distance close between Max and the silent monster. Despite his exhaustion, Max turned to face the thing that followed him.

With gloved hands, the monster lurched forward with its axe in tow, throwing its head back in delight at catching its prey. Its face paint was streaked by the rain, revealing flesh tones and scars in places washed clean by the relentless downpour. A black coat wrapped its body, but the figure was oddly rotund, a lumpy body strapped in place by tight criss-crossing belts that cut through the fabric and into the flesh. It hoisted the axe handle in both hands, preparing to bring the weapon up and over its head, ending the long chase.

"Who were you?" Max asked.

The mime paused, cocking its head, as though it had not heard a sane voice in centuries. Perhaps it hadn't.

"Who were you, before the stack fell?"

It shook its head, tightened its grip on its axe, and shuffled forward, grimacing with its mouth wide open. And Max saw then why it did not answer; its tongue had been severed, an old cut which had long since healed over with thick scars.

The imp on the wall top cackled and cracked its knuckles, a particularly human behavior. Had it also once been a resident of the stack?

Just as the monster heaved at its axe, the ground shook. On every side, walls cracked and crumbled, sending heavy stones rolling into the paths. The imp screamed as its perch collapsed, burying it under a pile of rubble. Max rushed forward and pulled at the clown-monster's belts, yanking at the buckles. As each one burst open, the creature came further undone; its lumpy body burst like infected cysts, gushing putrefaction onto the stone walkway.

Max ran, wiping his hands on the stone walls as he went. Despite the pain in his feet and the strain in his chest, he ran.

More hours passed. With his stalkers gone, Max had the

freedom to rest—yet still he ran on, with Penny's sobs ringing in his ears. Sometimes the tower loomed into view, but most of the time he could see only the walls, blocking out all but the darkness overhead which was streaked with bolts of violent electricity. His position in the maze was lit by an ambient glow like the kind you see in your dreams, coming from no particular source. There were no shadows and no reflections, just a cold blue light that illuminated his way around every corner he turned.

A dog barked sharply. It was to his left, no more than two sections away, and it had caught his scent.

Max stumbled on, but his resolve was fading. His enemies were closing in on their helpless prey. Another earthquake rocked the maze, sending more walls tumbling. Max chose a path through a newly created gap, and discovered an oversized hall, long enough to disappear into darkness on either end. The openness was intimidating, but at least he could see what was ahead—and what followed behind.

From the darkness emerged the hounds. They rushed forward, noses in the air, flashing white teeth. Each dog was the size of the mastiff from the upper levels of the stack; hundreds of pounds of meat and muscle, with the bulk of a golf cart. Their slick black pelts were covered in scars and fresh wounds, dripping spit and blood, ecstatic at finally viewing their quarry. And close behind them, Gleaner rushed through the hall, scraping his claws along the stone walls on either side, flaring his nostrils as he prepared to crush his prey.

"Jackal!" Gleaner yelled in a voice which boomed across the underworld, loud enough to cause fresh rockfalls to tumble from the tops of the labyrinth walls. "View halloo! Hounds, hie to the jackal! Pursue!"

Max scrambled through a wall opening too narrow

for the dogs to follow. They were forced to go around, but his ploy did not buy much time. If he had a play to make, it had to be now.

"Penny!" Max screamed. He had been discovered, and his death was imminent, but at least he could let Penny know he had never given up. Father was here, and she would not die alone. "Penny, where are you? Say my name if you can hear me!"

"Dad!" Penny called out. "I'm...over here! Follow my voice!"

Gleaner rounded the corner with his hounds. They had caught up quickly; Max ducked again through a crack in a wall. A new earthquake, stronger this time, shook the maze. The ground was bursting with the energy of the old god, but Gleaner's own power was working against him.

"Where are you? Say it again!"

"Here! Here!" Penny called out, over and over, as Max charged across the maze in a straight line. He was breaking the rules of the labyrinth—Gleaner's rules. It was time to stop letting the old god call all the shots. It was the only way to win.

"Keep it up!"

"Here...here..."

As Max rushed through each passage, he caught glimpses of Gleaner's horrifying collection of terrors. A stack of twitching skeletons filled one hall, the undead trapped forever in painful decay. In another, ponds of stinking acid ate away at everything they touched, eroding the flesh of the people and animals chained to its walls. Worshipers of the old god shuddered against the stones, cradling severed limbs they had cut away to prove their loyalty or to win Gleaner's approval. At every turn, Max found another display of the mad old god's arrogance and cruelty.

Gleaner roared. His quarry was too small and quick. The howling was followed by a crash, and more tumbling rock; Gleaner had leapt to the wall-tops, skipping across the maze in a route to match Max's own.

But Max had nearly reached the tower. He could finally view it unobstructed, standing tall on its hilltop, with its flat roof visible over the walls. Gleaner was gaining ground fast; only minutes remained before Max was overtaken. The bear breathed in heavy gusts, expelling low grunts of anger and anticipation as it bounded from wall to wall.

"Dad!" Penny screamed. "Here!"

Max could see her now, reaching her arms out through the bars. He climbed up the slope, fumbling through falling chunks of rocks and pulverized sand which were the remains of maze walls shaken apart by tremors over millennia. Colliding on each side of the gate, father and daughter embraced. Max jammed his arms as far through the bars as he could, and Penny wrapped her arms around his middle.

"It's locked," Penny sobbed. "I can't get out."

The sight of the massive bear progressing across the labyrinth was mesmerizing in its monstrosity; the creature's claws crumbled the walls as it went. It disregarded the destruction of its own creation in single-minded pursuit of its prey. Bloody-pink spray was expelled from its flaring nostrils with every leap, illuminated by the fiery glow from its eyes. Gleaner was two hundred feet away, then only a hundred. Max was out of time.

Gleaner looked up at the tower and bellowed with rage at the sight of Max embracing Penny. Another earthquake, larger than any which preceded it, rocked the maze. Its magnitude seemed to be fed by the old god's anger. The gate to Penny's prison creaked in its frame as it shook, while gaps appeared on each side in time with the swaying ground. It gave Max an idea.

"Push! Penny, before the shaking stops, push hard! I'll pull!"

Together, they wrenched the gate loose before the earthquake started to ebb. The bars gave way suddenly, sending Max tumbling back down the hill before he could catch his feet. By the time he returned to Penny at the tower, Gleaner had arrived. The creature stood atop the last wall and roared in victory, spewing spit from its open mouth. It quieted and stared, unblinking, at the intruders.

"You lose," Gleaner said.

Max held Penny tight. She sobbed into his chest, wetting his shirt with her tears.

The bear jumped to the ground and stood up on its hind legs as the final, midnight earthquake began. Far, far overhead, a rumbling signaled the dropping of the stack. The house was sinking, descending toward Gleaner's hellish depths. The bear grew larger, its hulking body expanding until it was thirty feet tall, bellowing and crying out with pleasure at its own infernal power.

Penny went limp in Max's arms as she lost hope. His own resolve started to drain away, and his senses dulled. His body felt wispy, ghostlike. A fog of resignation clouded his vision, and Penny's grip on his torso loosened. They began to drift apart. As the stack far above them collapsed, Max and Penny started to die.

"No," he whispered. "Please…"

"You are bound to me," the old god groaned. "Come, now. It is already done."

Max's blood slowed and cooled as Gleaner spoke the words. His feet felt like lead weights, no longer painful but made of stone like the labyrinth itself. His bones fused, becoming rigid, and his skin hardened; his flesh was turning to rock.

Penny's skin took on a pallor as it was dusted with granite powder. Her hair dulled, and her eyes turned to marble. In minutes they would both be statues, trapped in the calcified forms of their own bodies, locked in forever. Never able to speak or touch, but only look on as Gleaner committed his atrocities for years to come.

"No!" Max screamed, forcing his joints to work. Crumbles of dust popped from the inside creases of his elbows, where the flesh had already fused together. "Leave us alone!" He arched his back, working it free of the creeping clay. He held Penny tight, and his embrace snapped a coating of crusted rock from her skin. It fell away like a carapace but grew back again as quickly as it broke, reaching up her body, regaining its hold.

"Fight back, Penny," Max whispered in her ear. "Don't let it take you. Hold me tight, and if you feel it taking over, hold me even tighter."

Gleaner transformed into his wapiti form, and laughed. Brash, human laughter from the elk's bleeding mouth echoed through the labyrinth walls, mocking Max's dying efforts. The earthquakes continued, rocking and rolling. The hounds, finally catching up to their prey, bounded from an opening in the wall. But they calmed and sat near their master when they saw that the blood of their quarry had dried up. There was nothing left to hunt here, only statues with darting eyes and pounding hearts.

"You cannot defeat a god, Mr. Braun," Gleaner said. "I am more ancient than you can imagine. I am dying, but the life of a god is not measured by the human standard. I have centuries ahead of me. You could have, too, if not for your arrogance. If only you had been less trouble, I might have let you stay in your old home, like all the rest. You could have had so much more *time*."

Max could not respond. His tongue was a rock, and

his teeth felt like smooth river-pebbles. The ongoing quake shook him from side to side, threatening to topple the single figure that he and Penny now comprised. But he used the last of his remaining strength to snap his right arm free of the encroaching stony growth, and he bent his elbow. If he was to be a statue for all of eternity, he would do it on his own terms. In his final seconds of freedom, he turned up his hand, made a fist, and raised his middle finger.

Gleaner howled. "You spoiled it! Ruined my new statue! I'll crush you! I'll…" The elk stomped, trampling the floor, and the earthquake increased. Far overhead, something creaked, then cracked. There was a tearing and a rain of cement powder, a splash of water, a stream of dust and dirt and debris. From the distant ceiling, something worked itself free.

The stack was falling.

Booming in the darkness, the long shaft of the structure came unmoored like a molar from rotten gums. As it fell, a high, maniacal laughter rang out in the storm; Desmond hung out from a smashed window, howling with vindication, riding the building down on its final descent into Hell. It plummeted toward the labyrinth, whistling in the wind, and smashed into Gleaner, plunging the old god's body deep into the earth with an explosion of concrete and fury. Chunks of plaster shot into the air, mixed with the pouring rain, and came back down as sodden clumps of clay. When the structure settled in its final resting place, the remains of the stack lay in a massive heap with the broken bones of its shattered wooden beams sticking up from the rubble.

A hush fell over the maze. Writhing, agonized souls went still. Screaming animals quieted, lowering their heads with relief. All the tortured beings whose lives Gleaner had painfully extended were released as his power waned.

Max felt the spreading petrifaction retreat, loosening his limbs. Penny's arms fell to her sides, becoming flesh once again, and she looked up at Max's face as tears streamed from her eyes, clearing the white ash and dust from her skin in streaks. She whispered, "Is he dead?"

"I don't think so. I don't know if anything can kill an old god. But his strength has been weakened enough to release his prisoners, and that's enough for now. He might be back some day, but not in my lifetime, or in yours."

CHAPTER 26 – The Wapiti of 1989

It was funny, Max thought, that no matter how horrific an experience in your past might have been, time had a way of smoothing it over and softening the edges until even the worst days of your life became shrouded with passive nostalgia. It's not that you forget how awful the bad times were, or have any real desire to relive them. But perhaps the longing you feel is more for yourself, for the person you used to be. That younger version of you, who was fighting their battle and winning their war—which, in hindsight, did not kill you after all.

Max bought a rocking chair. It made him feel somewhat old and stodgy, but the seat was so comfortable he couldn't resist. It sat on the cedar wood deck that overlooked the front yard, an addition he added halfway through construction after a flash of inspiration. The new house was built adjacent to the sinkhole. From his chair he could keep an eye on the pit, listening to the low howl of wind whipping across the gaping hole. He had built a fence around it which matched the deer fence that bordered the property, ostensibly to keep anyone from falling in—but of course, it was really to stop anything from getting out.

Not that there had been any problems so far. Ten years had passed since the stack had fallen, and only wind moved within the hole that remained. The new house was situated on the north side near the trees, slightly elevated above the pit, with a good view of the entire property. Where the lot could be watched.

After Max had contracted the pouring of the concrete slab, he had been able to finish much of the remaining

construction work himself. Penny had helped him on
weekends, holding drywall in place, painting the walls in
eggshell white. They had lost everything when the stack
fell, but Max had always been a believer in insurance, and
they were able to scrape by until the house was rebuilt
with the payout. The insurance company had squabbled a
bit about the loss of the house to a sinkhole, saying it was
an uncovered "Act of God." They were closer to the truth
than they knew, but in the end the company came through
with the money.

In 1986, Penny went off to college. It hurt Max to let
her go, deeper than he was willing to admit, but he loved
her too much to discourage her. He also knew that she
needed to get away from the property. She had never trust-
ed the pit, never even got near it. But Max refused to move
away. 23 Old Mine Road was the first home he had ever
owned, and he was determined to remain its caretaker.

After the stack fell, the mail started showing up reg-
ularly. Bills, pamphlets, jury duty. Mr. Samson retired and
was replaced by Miss Maloney, a lovely woman who Max
took out on a few dates.

By day, Max continued to craft and sell miniatures. In
the evening, he watched the pit. Nothing went in, nothing
came out. But it became his habit to guard it. After what
he had seen in the depths, he would take no chances.

Midsummer Day of 1989 was hot. Boiling, searing, scorching hot. Penny had called on the phone and failed to con-
vince Max to leave for the day. She was full of good ideas;
Dad could take a trip up to the mountains, or he could
rent a beach house and watch the ocean for a while instead
of the pit. Maybe treat himself to a night in a swanky hotel
in San Francisco, or book a week at a gorgeous resort up
north where she had stayed with her friends last year.

Anything—anything at all—other than stay on the property on Midsummer Night.

Max was unswayed. Of all the nights of his endless
watch, this one would be the most important. If nothing
happened, then Gleaner really was gone. But if there was a
disturbance, Max needed to be there. Penny pleaded, but
Max refused. He would not turn his back on the pit. He
dissuaded Penny from coming home; she was on summer
break in Los Angeles with friends, but when she suggested
she could sit with him and be ready to help in case something happened, he forbade it. She pretended to be disappointed when Max refused, but he could hear the relief in
her voice. Her experience with Gleaner had traumatized
her, and Max would never let her be hurt by him again.

So on June 24, 1989, he was alone. He adopted a
festive mood to counter his nervousness. For dinner, he
grilled hot dogs on a charcoal barbecue, and corn from
the farmer's market. For dessert, a big bowl of ice cream
paired with his favorite bourbon—limited to one glass,
these days. Classic tunes blasted on the radio to drown out
the dark silence from the pit. Rhombus, a Basset hound
he had rescued from the pound two years ago, sat nearby,
gnawing on an old hambone.

Life was good.

Due to the anniversary, his mind insisted on wandering back to the events of ten years ago, mulling over
past mistakes, turning over the bodies. There were three,
planted right there on the hillside, weren't there? The two
workmen, and that lady from the collections agency. No
one ever came looking for them, or perhaps Gleaner had
scared off any nosy inquirers before they got close enough
to ask. Years later, in 1983 or 1984, Max had fashioned
three exquisite wooden markers to place at the heads of
the graves. No etchings or names on them, of course, but

they were polished and lacquered, built to last for decades. He had read Bible verses at the graves despite not being religiously inclined, in case any of the three interred were Christian. He had done what he could, within reason.

But you never sought their families, did you? You could have at least done that.

Max shook his head. Some days the accusatory voices in his head were louder than others. But he hadn't killed those people. Gleaner had. And that was something Max could never explain to an outsider.

The new house was smaller than the original had been, but more directly suited to his purposes. There were only two bedrooms, and when Penny moved out his workshop moved from an outside shed into her old room. When she visited now, she had to sleep on the sofa—but there was no hatch under it, so Max didn't worry. All was well, and she didn't mind the sofa one bit. She was still young.

As the sun started to set on the evening of Midsummer Day, Max rocked. His chair never creaked or complained; it was well-made by a top craftsman in Roseville. A blue sedan drove past, and its driver waved. Mrs. Hutchison, from up the hill. Nice lady. She had two fluffy white Pomeranians, and a grandson in law school. All the neighbors were nice enough, although they sensed there was something strange about the sinkhole. Max chatted with them after city council meetings or in the grocery store parking lot, but they would never visit him at his home. That was just as well. Max was a private man.

A breeze picked up, shaking the boughs of the pine trees. A crow cawed, a rough and raspy cry, as it soared high over the house's angled roof. Max ate his hot dogs with dill relish and a yellow snake of dijon mustard. He balanced the paper plate in his lap, and tossed little bits of meat to Rhombus. It was a beautiful evening.

Hours passed, and all was still. Of course it was. Why
wouldn't it be? Gleaner had been crushed. He was little
more than a twisted bulb planted deep in the ground
under his own hell, interred by the stack itself. He was
killed by the combined efforts of Max and Penny and the
old god's own immense power. Desmond had helped too,
probably—at least he had been there, at the last, laughing
in his strange high voice.

"Half an hour to go," Max told Rhombus. His watch
said 11:28. Thirty-two minutes until nothing happened,
and he could go to bed.

From the forest stepped an elk. It was an enormous
creature, the largest animal Max had seen in a decade. Its
rack of antlers was seven feet wide, tip to tip. Max ducked
to the boards of the deck, hiding behind the railing.

"Rhombus! Here, inside! Get inside, boy," he whispered. The dog dropped its bone and plodded through the
front door without noticing the elk.

Max followed the dog in on all fours as his mind
raced, making plans. The shotgun was loaded and ready
on the coffee table. He had prepared it for use but kept
it inside, in case a neighbor drove by. He didn't want to
alarm someone over nothing.

But it wasn't nothing, was it? Gleaner was here. It had
to be him; no other animal was that large, not in these
sparse suburban woods. Max was astonished the old god
had returned after ten years of peace, but his presence
outside was undeniable.

He crawled through the living room, gripping the
shotgun in one hand. After locking Rhombus in the
bedroom, Max crept back through the house, crouching to
stay below the level of the windows. Popping his head up

to the glass, he spotted the elk as it made its way across the lot towards the pit. It moved with a slow, hypnotized gait, as if it was being drawn in by a low voice. Max slid the window open and rested the barrel of the gun on the sill, aiming at the elk. It was a perfect shot. But he couldn't pull the trigger.

Something was wrong. The elk looked lost, almost pitiable. It was fully grown, but moved with the gangly awkwardness of a faun, stumbling as it approached the fence around the sinkhole. It put its head over the top rail and peered into the hole with a vacant stare.

The elk was broadside to the house. Max couldn't miss. He willed his trigger finger to press down, take the shot, kill the monster. Instead, he tucked the gun under his arm and walked out the front door. The elk didn't turn as Max walked down the steps. It gazed into the pit, mesmer-ized, shifting its weight back and forth on its hooves.

"Gleaner," Max said.

The elk turned its head. Its muzzle was dry, clean of blood. And its eyes were not red, but ruddy brown. It almost looked like a normal animal.

Yet the elk was not frightened. It wasn't just a wild creature; Max sensed there was something else, deep inside, that was broken and bent. It turned its head to one side to examine him, flaring its nostrils at his scent. And it was then that Max saw its pupil, in the shape of a diamond.

"So, it really is you," Max said. "But also not. What are you?"

The elk did not speak, but Max knew the answer. Nothing could kill an old god. Gleaner was here, but he was weak—and perhaps he did not even remember who he was anymore. But some day the old god would wake up from his healing dream, and would remember his own power. And then he would start collecting people again.

"You are not welcome here," Max said. "And you never will be. This land is mine. I am bound to it. You can no longer lay claim."

The elk shook its head, sending a flurry of gnats into the air. For a moment, a flicker of lucidity danced in its eye. Gleaner saw Max, understood his words. A long drop of spittle spilled from the elk's lower lip.

Max raised his gun to his shoulder and aimed it at the elk's diamond eye. "Last chance, Gleaner. This land is mine. Leave this place and never come back, or I'll blow your brains out and you will have to start your last ten years of recovery from the beginning again."

The elk stared down the barrel of the gun and opened its mouth in a laugh. Its mocking bray echoed through the forest, and the wild animals in the pines called back in a cacophony of wolf howls and bird calls and the roaring of bears. As the forest came alive, the elk reared back, kicking its front hooves. It lurched, launching its body over the fence, and plummeted into the hole.

As Max watched the elk's bloody rump disappear into the darkness, he was overcome with regret. He should have shot the elk. But it had been his foolish hope that Gleaner would actually leave. Max knew he could not kill the mad old god. Peace would only last if one of them moved on from this place. And that would never happen.

Max returned to his rocking chair and sat down with a groan, stretching out his stiff legs. He balanced the shotgun on his knees, and took up his watch. Rhombus returned to his place at Max's side, picking up his hambone again. For the first time, a strong desire to give up and leave the property rose within Max; he could just walk away, forget it all, and never come back. Penny had moved out, and Emily was long gone. Nothing was stopping him now.

But how strong would Gleaner be in another ten years? Another twenty? If Max left, someone else would become a victim. More families, like Mickey and his parents. Or sad, lonely men like Desmond—or like himself. No, he could never leave. As Gleaner had once proclaimed, Max was bound, just as snared as he would have been if he had collapsed with the stack. He was free to leave, but the knowledge of the trap he had left for others to stumble into would follow him for the rest of his life.

No, he would stay. He would stay and make sure Gleaner collected no more souls.

"Ten years go to," Max told Rhombus. "Just another ten years. Then he'll be back. And then we'll see what's what."

If you enjoyed this book, please leave a review!

Independent authors can not keep writing awesome books unless readers leave reviews. If you want to support writers, leave your opinion or rating wherever you found this book so others can learn from your experience.

You can also sign up for my newsletter at www.ccluckey. com and get early access to FREE short stories, information on becoming part of my limited advance reader team, and updates on my upcoming new releases.

Thank you for reading!

C.C. Luckey writes uniquely imaginative and eerie stories influenced by her studies for degree in Philosophy. Prior to beginning her writing career, she spent many years working as a costumer for a variety of productions ranging from volunteer theater troupes to Hollywood feature films. As a multi-talented actor and musician, she has had many unique experiences including performing on stage to sold-out Los Angeles amphitheaters, extensive cross-country travel, and playing live music to an audience of millions on national television. She lives in Long Beach, California in a 100-year-old house with her husband and two corgi dogs. Follow C.C. Luckey at her web site (www.ccluckey.com) for free content, information on how to become part of a limited advance reader team, and updates on new releases. She can also be found on Facebook at @ccluckey and Twitter @ ccluckey_author.